The Secrets of the Fear Family . . .

The history of the Fear family is a dark and strange one, filled with death, madness, tragic love, and revenge.

No one can escape the curse of the Fear family. Simon Fear tried. He changed the spelling of his family name from Fier to Fear and tried to start a new life. But he could not hide from his destiny—the Fear curse destroyed his entire family.

Except one. Nicholas Fear. The child of Daniel Fear and Nora Goode.

Will this new Fear be the one to break the curse? Or will he suffer the fate of his doomed family?

Books by R. L. Stine

Fear Street
THE NEW GIRL
THE SURPRISE PARTY
THE OVERNIGHT
MISSING
THE WRONG NUMBER
THE SLEEPWALKER
HAUNTED
HALLOWEEN PARTY
THE STEPSISTER
SKI WEEKEND
THE FIRE GAME
LIGHTS OUT
THE SECRET BEDROOM
THE KNIFE
PROM QUEEN
FIRST DATE
THE BEST FRIEND
THE CHEATER
SUNBURN
THE NEW BOY
THE DARE
BAD DREAMS
DOUBLE DATE
THE THRILL CLUB
ONE EVIL SUMMER
THE MIND READER
WRONG NUMBER 2
TRUTH OR DARE
DEAD END
FINAL GRADE
SWITCHED
COLLEGE WEEKEND
THE STEPSISTER 2
WHAT HOLLY HEARD
THE FACE
SECRET ADMIRER

Fear Street Super Chillers
PARTY SUMMER
SILENT NIGHT
GOODNIGHT KISS
BROKEN HEARTS
SILENT NIGHT 2
THE DEAD LIFEGUARD
CHEERLEADERS: THE NEW EVIL
BAD MOONLIGHT
THE NEW YEAR'S PARTY

The Fear Street Saga
THE BETRAYAL
THE SECRET
THE BURNING

Fear Street Cheerleaders
THE FIRST EVIL
THE SECOND EVIL
THE THIRD EVIL

99 Fear Street: The House of Evil
THE FIRST HORROR
THE SECOND HORROR
THE THIRD HORROR

The Cataluna Chronicles
THE EVIL MOON
THE DARK SECRET
THE DEADLY FIRE

Fear Street Sagas
A NEW FEAR

Other Novels
HOW I BROKE UP WITH ERNIE
PHONE CALLS
CURTAINS
BROKEN DATE

Available from ARCHWAY Paperbacks

FEAR STREET SAGAS® #1

R·L·STINE

A New Fear

A Parachute Press Book

AN ARCHWAY PAPERBACK
Published by POCKET BOOKS
New York London Toronto Sydney Tokyo Singapore

AN ARCHWAY PAPERBACK *Original*

An Archway Paperback published by
POCKET BOOKS, a division of Simon & Schuster Inc.
1230 Avenue of the Americas, New York, NY 10020

ISBN: 0-671-52952-8

First Archway Paperback printing March 1996

10 9 8 7 6 5 4 3 2 1

Cover art by Lisa Falkenstern

Printed in the U.S.A.

IL 7+

R. L. Stine wishes to thank
Brandon Alexander
for his contributions and efforts
on this manuscript.

Prologue

The Village of Shadyside
1900

Nora Goode Fear bowed her head. Tired, so very tired. She had been sitting in this cold room most of the night, answering questions. Describing everything she had witnessed at the Fear mansion.

Not once.

Not twice.

But three times now.

And still they held her prisoner here. In this room without windows. In this room that held more darkness than light.

The flame of a solitary candle flickered. The shadows shifted.

Nora lifted her gaze to the man sitting behind the desk. He alone would determine her fate. He had the authority to set her free. He had the power to lock her away.

The man sighed heavily and leaned back in his

chair. He scattered papers before him. Papers containing his questions and her answers.

Nora wiped the tears from her eyes and straightened her spine. She tried to swallow, but her throat was too dry. Her back ached. She was hungry and tired. She wanted to slide out of the chair, curl up on the floor, and go to sleep.

She wanted to dream of Daniel, her husband of one day. Of the happy times they shared before his family's curse brought them death and destruction.

"All right, Nora," the man said sternly. "Tell me again what happened."

Again? Nora's shoulders slumped forward. If I am not insane now, she thought wearily, I soon will be. How can I keep telling this tale of horror over and over? I want to forget all that happened, but he forces me to remember.

Impatiently, the man rapped on the desk with his knuckles. "Tell me the truth about what happened at the Fear mansion. Tell me the truth and you shall be released."

I must be strong, Nora thought. Strong for my baby. Daniel's and mine.

Nora knew she carried Daniel Fear's child. Knew it in her heart. She would do anything to protect their baby. Anything.

She swallowed hard and forced herself to answer calmly. "Daniel's grandfather, Simon Fear, was celebrating his seventy-fifth birthday. All the candles on the cake were burning. Daniel announced that Nora

Goode Fear was his new wife. His grandfather screamed—"

"Liar!" the man cried. "You were never married. Everyone in Shadyside knows that."

"We were married!" Nora protested. How could she convince the man to believe her?

"Our marriage was a secret," Nora explained. "We did not want to tell our families until after the ceremony. We were afraid they would try to stop us—because of the feud between the Fears and the Goodes."

The man shook his head, his lips pressed together in a thin line. "Go on," he said impatiently.

"Daniel and I eloped. We did not even take the time to choose wedding rings. Daniel gave me this instead." Nora lifted the chain of the amulet she wore around her neck.

"That night was Daniel's grandfather's seventy-fifth birthday. Someone brought in a cake with all the candles lit. Then Daniel announced our marriage. His grandfather screamed and rose from his wheelchair—"

"Impossible!" the man barked. "Simon Fear was a weak old man. He could not rise from his wheelchair."

Nora flinched at his harsh tone. "But he did," Nora insisted. "Then he fell and crashed onto the table. The cake toppled off. The flames from the candles started the fire."

"You expect me to believe that the tiny candles on a

birthday cake burned an enormous mansion to the ground?"

Nora squeezed her eyes shut and nodded. She could see Daniel standing by her side and introducing her to his grandparents. The next moment, a wall of fire separated them—forever.

"You did not try to put out the fire?" the man asked.

"No one could put out the fire. Daniel tried, but it was like a living, breathing thing. A thing with a will of its own. So hot and bright."

Nora took a deep breath and forced herself to meet the man's cold eyes. "And I saw faces—laughing, screaming faces—in the flames," she said firmly.

Nora felt more tears begin to flow down her cheeks. She dashed them away.

"Enough!" The man pounded his fist on the table. "I gave you four opportunities to tell the truth. The events you describe are impossible."

He picked up a pen, dipped it in an inkwell, and scrawled his name across the paper. The candle flame wavered. Shadows danced across the man's face.

He lifted his eyes and captured her gaze. "I am sorry, Nora, but I have no choice. I must declare you insane and commit you to the insane asylum."

Nora opened her lips and uttered an anguished cry that echoed through the room.

PART ONE

Chapter 1

The Village of Shadyside
1901

Nora hated the night.

During the day, she heard a cry or two from down the hall. She heard a thump above her cell or a bump below.

But at night, deep moans and screams reverberated off the walls of the asylum. Nora covered her ears, but she could still hear the cries of the other inmates.

What do they see in their nightmares? Nora wondered. *Can it be more horrible than what I see through my window?*

Nora peered through the black iron bars. Just as she had every night for ten long months now. The ten long months she had been locked in the asylum.

Beyond the bars she could make out the remains of the Fear mansion against the full moon. How could any nightmare be more terrifying than that?

Nora noticed the workers had made more progress on the road running through the Fear property.

A road they would call Fear Street.

Nora wrapped her arms around her body. She had tried to tell the doctors and nurses that the road was a bad idea. They would not listen.

Why would they? They thought she was insane.

But she knew the bad luck that surrounded the Fears had somehow seeped into their land. Tainted it.

She turned from the window. The darkness always came too swiftly, wrapping shadows around the bed, the table, the chair.

And the cradle.

Bending, Nora lifted her son into her arms. Nicholas gazed at her with trusting brown eyes . . . his father's eyes. Daniel Fear's eyes.

She returned to the window and sat on the wooden floor. Wind whistled through the cracked glass. Nora leaned forward and breathed deeply. The fresh night air reminded her of the world outside. The world she wanted Nicholas to know.

But her son had been born in this place. He had never been outside the iron bars and locked doors of the insane asylum.

Nora preferred to sleep leaning against the window, holding her son. Her mattress stank of stale perfume, blood, sweat, and death. She never used it.

She rocked back and forth. Someone screamed—a high shrill sound. Her son cried softly. Looking at his innocent face, Nora brushed the brown hair away from his furrowed brow.

"It is only the wind. Only the wind," she whispered. "I will take care of you. Do not worry. I will always take care of you."

Nora felt the warmth of the sunlight on her eyelids. Slowly, she opened her eyes.

Another day.

Keys rattled as someone unlocked the door. Nicholas whimpered, and Nora picked him up and held him close.

The door burst open. A large woman stood in the doorway. Martha, Nora's nurse. Her body blocked the light from the hallway. "It is time for your bath, Nora."

Martha stepped aside. A young girl darted into the room. "Nancy will watch the babe," Martha said.

Nancy wore a coarse white cotton shift like Nora's. It identified her as an inmate of the asylum. She waved her hands frantically before her, an empty smile frozen on her face. "Baby. I watch baby."

Nora hugged Nicholas tighter. "Could a nurse stay with him?"

"Nancy is twelve. Certainly old enough to watch a baby," Martha snapped.

"Twelve," Nancy repeated as she held out her arms.

"He's sleeping," Nora lied as she placed Nicholas in the cradle.

"Sleeping," Nancy said. She sounded disappointed, but her smile remained.

"You must *not* hold him while he's sleeping," Nora said.

"Must *not* hold him," Nancy repeated as she stared into the cradle.

"Just watch him and keep him safe," Nora added softly.

"Watch him and keep him safe," Nancy mimicked. She began to rock the cradle and sing a lullaby.

Reluctantly, Nora followed Martha from the room. Martha slammed the door shut and locked it. She wrapped a beefy hand around Nora's arm and forced her down the stairs.

When they entered the first floor, Nora saw a man banging his head against the wall. "It hurts," he said. And banged his head again. "It hurts."

A woman sitting in a corner clawed at her face with her fingernails. Bright red blood covered her hands.

Martha charged over to the woman, jerking Nora with her. She grabbed the woman's wrist. "Stop it! Stop it, Charlotte!"

"I need to get them off," the woman whined.

"Orderly! Tie this woman to her bed!" Martha shouted.

"I have to get the spiders off. They are biting me. Biting my face," the woman wailed.

A young man rushed over and picked Charlotte up as if she were a child. He carried her down the hallway. "I need to get them off," the woman cried again and again.

Martha tightened her grip on Nora's arm and stomped toward the stairway leading to the basement. Nora stumbled as Martha yanked her down the stairs.

Martha opened the door and shoved Nora inside

the dark, damp room. Nora pressed her back to the wall. She hated coming here.

Martha pushed open another door. "Get inside."

Nora held her breath as she entered the room. The light was dim. A scrawny woman with loose skin hanging from her bones stepped out of the cast-iron bathtub. Open sores covered her shivering body. Her teeth chattered.

Nora knew the water was cold. The water was always cold. And the room had no fire to warm it.

An attendant wrapped a blanket around the thin woman and guided her out of the room.

Nora released her breath and the room's foul odors rushed into her nose. Sweat, decay, mold. She always felt dirtier after a bath in this room.

"Hurry along," Martha instructed. "You do not want Nancy to play with your son too long."

Shivering after her bath, Nora followed Martha back to her room. She had dried off, but still she felt damp.

Martha slipped her key into the lock, turned it, and shoved the door open. Nora rushed in.

Nancy stood by the cradle, rocking it back and forth. "Say bye-bye," she muttered. "Nancy say bye-bye to baby."

Nora studied her son. His eyes were closed. He slept peacefully.

"Come along, Nancy," Martha ordered from the doorway.

"Come along," Nancy repeated in a singsong voice.

Nancy trotted toward the door. Then she spun back to face the cradle. "Nancy say bye-bye. Baby go to new home now. Baby go to new home."

"What?" Nora gasped. She clasped her hands together to keep them from trembling. "What, Nancy?"

"Nancy say bye-bye to baby," Nancy answered. She nodded her head up and down, up and down.

Slowly Nora raised her eyes to meet Martha's. "No," she whispered.

"Yes," Martha answered firmly. "Nancy is correct. The baby cannot be raised in an insane asylum. He is almost old enough to leave you. They will take him soon."

Chapter 2

"When?" Nora yelled. "When will they come for Nicholas?" She had to know. She needed to make plans. She would never allow anyone to take Nicholas from her.

"Calm yourself," Martha ordered. "They will come when they come. Screaming your throat raw will not change anything."

Nora grabbed Martha's arm. "What will they do to him? Where will they take him? Please tell me. You must."

Martha pried Nora's fingers off her arm. "That is enough," she ordered. "I do not want to have you restrained."

Martha made her way to the door. "Wherever they take the baby, he will be better off," she said over her shoulder.

But he will not have me, Nora thought. He will not

have his own mother. And no one else could love Nicholas the way I do.

The moment Martha locked the door behind her, Nora reached under her mattress and pulled out the rope.

She rubbed it between her fingers. Still not thick enough. And she had been working on it for months.

Nora unbraided her hair and shook it free. It fell almost to her knees.

She separated several strands and jerked them out, ignoring the irritating pain in her scalp.

She wove the hair into her makeshift rope. A rope made of hair, threads from her blanket, threads from her clothes, and anything else she could find.

Nora tried to be gentle as she plucked more hair, but her hands shook. She felt afraid. Afraid they would come too soon. Afraid they would come and take Nicholas away before she was ready.

When she finished the rope, Nora planned to push the chair leg against the cracked corner of the window until the glass gave way. Then she would bundle Nicholas in a blanket, tie the rope around his protected body, and slowly lower him to the ground.

Next she would douse the fire in the hearth and climb up the chimney until she reached the roof. Somehow from there she would find a way to the ground and Nicholas.

Nora rehearsed the escape plan over and over in her mind as she added to the soft rope. The plan had to work. It had to.

The wind howled outside. Nora stopped her work

to listen more carefully. She heard another sound mingle with the sound of the wind.

Someone calling for help! Nora sprang to the window and peered out. She saw one of the doctors run down the front steps. A red-haired boy dashed over to him.

"There has been an accident!" the boy yelled. "A bad one. On that road they are making by the Fear mansion. Three men crushed!"

If only they had listened to her. Nora knew the dark forces of the Fear family would claim more lives. She knew the road would only bring disaster to the town.

Nicholas whimpered softly. Nora lifted him into her arms and rocked him gently. The evil Fear legacy would never touch her son, she promised herself. Never.

The baby drifted back to sleep, and Nora returned him to his cradle. Then she reached up and grabbed another clump of her hair. She yanked it out, gritting her teeth against the pain.

She had to get Nicholas away from this horrible place. Away from the asylum. Away from the town. Away from everything tainted by the Fears.

Nora wove the hairs into the rope. She grabbed another bunch of hair and tore it out.

She felt the warm, wet blood trickle down her cheek. She did not care. All she cared about was Nicholas.

Nora added the hairs to the rope with trembling fingers.

She gazed into the cradle. "Do not worry, Nicholas," she crooned. "I will take care of you. I will not let them take you from me. Not ever."

The door flew open with a bang.

Nora gasped.

"What are you doing, Nora?" a low voice demanded.

Chapter 3

Nora jerked her head toward the door. Her doctor stood there watching her. She had not heard him enter.

The doctor strode to Nora. "What is this?" he asked, pulling the long, silky braid from her hands.

Nora fought to remain calm. "Since you took away my pen and writing paper, I have nothing to do. The braid is simply a way to occupy my time."

The doctor wound the rope of hair around his hand. "Very clever, Nora. Did you think to escape with this flimsy rope?"

"No!" she insisted. "But I do not belong in this awful place."

"That is for me to decide," he said. He pulled out his handkerchief and wiped a streak of blood from Nora's forehead.

The doctor strode to the door and opened it. "Send

Martha to me," he called down the hall. "And tell her to bring the scissors."

"No," Nora whimpered, tears filling her eyes. "Please, no."

Nicholas began to cry. Nora scooped him up and held him tightly.

Moments later Martha stalked into the room.

"Nora has been pulling out her hair to make a rope," the doctor informed Martha. "Cut it off."

"Of course, Doctor." Martha gave him a wide smile.

"Come, Nora," Martha crooned as she held up a large pair of scissors. She opened and closed them several times. The tinny sound set Nora's teeth on edge. "It is for the best. We cannot have you pulling your hair out by the roots. We cannot have you hurting yourself."

"I will never do it again," Nora promised, backing away.

Martha slipped the scissors into the pocket of her uniform and held out her arms. "Give me your son. I'll put him to bed."

I could run, Nora thought frantically. I could dart between Martha and the doctor before they know what I have in mind. I could be out of this room, down the stairs, and away from the asylum before anyone caught me.

And if they grab me? Nicholas might get hurt, she realized. Martha might accidentally stab him with the scissors. Or I might drop him.

He is innocent. I must protect him. Now is not the time to fight. But the time to fight will come.

Defeated for the moment, Nora tenderly placed her son in Martha's arms. She watched Martha return the baby to his cradle.

"Now, move closer to the hearth, so I can see what I am doing," Martha snapped.

Nora walked to the hearth and sank to the floor. Folding her hands in her lap, she waited.

Martha grabbed a fistful of Nora's hair and yanked it up. Nora bit her lip to stifle a cry of pain.

The scissors snipped. The tinny sound grated on Nora's nerves. A lock of her long, dark hair fell into her lap. Daniel loved my hair, Nora thought numbly.

She stared into the fire as the weight on her head lightened. Martha jerked her head as she cut, but Nora would not complain.

How would Nora escape now? Without her long hair, she would never be able to weave another rope. And soon they would come to take her son away.

Nora lifted her eyes and stared at the doctor. He stared back, his eyes cold, his face expressionless. Nora knew tears and pleading would have no effect on him. He would not help her keep Nicholas.

The cold steel scissors touched her scalp and Nora shivered. She did not dare reach up to see if she had any hair left.

Martha gathered her shorn hair and tossed it into the fire. The flames in the hearth hissed and crackled. Smoke drifted into the room. The odor of singed hair stung Nora's nostrils.

"I hope you learned your lesson," Martha said. "You are without power here. Cause us any more trouble, and you will regret it."

Nora held back her tears until she heard Martha and the doctor leave the room, locking the door behind them.

Then she bowed her head and released a wail of despair. I must find a way to escape before insanity claims my mind, she thought.

Against her will, her fingers touched the bristly remains of her hair. How could anyone look at me now and not see a madwoman? she wondered as she buried her face in her hands. When will this nightmare end?

Harsh voices in the hallway woke Nora. She rose from the floor, tiptoed across the room, and pressed her ear against the hard oak door.

"She probably cried herself to sleep," a scratchy voice murmured. Nora recognized the voice of the doctor.

"What will we do when Nora tells people?" another voice asked.

"Who will believe her? We will simply explain she killed the baby and we buried him. Who do you think they will believe? An insane woman? Or a respected doctor?"

Nora backed away from the door. She glanced around the barren room. She had no weapons, no way to protect Nicholas.

She walked to his cradle and lifted him into her

arms. "Our journey to safety will begin soon, Nicholas. I don't know how we will manage it, but we *will* find a way to escape."

He gurgled and smiled at her. Tears stung her eyes. He trusted her. She would not disappoint him.

She walked to the window. Holding Nicholas close, she waited.

Sweat popped out on her forehead. She wiped it away impatiently. She heard the key go into the lock.

"They're coming," she whispered. "They're coming."

Nicholas cooed. She tightened her hold on him. "I must convince them we don't belong here," she said softly. She looked at her son. "It is wrong to lie, Nicholas, but I am desperate. To save you, I will do anything."

Bowing her head, she kissed his soft cheek. "When you grow up, always tell the truth."

Metal ground against metal as the key turned.

Silence filled the room.

Seconds ticked by like minutes.

The knob turned.

The hinges squeaked.

The door slowly opened.

The doctor and two large assistants stood in the shadows.

Escape was impossible.

Nora stepped into the center of the room. She straightened her back, tilted up her chin, and met the doctor's questioning gaze.

"I lied the night you questioned me. You were right.

There were no ghosts that night. No screaming faces in the flames. The only screams I heard were my own."

Nora rushed on. "I know the truth. The Fears possess no dark powers. There is no curse on the family. There is nothing wrong with building a road on Fear property. No one in Shadyside is in danger."

"I am proud of you, Nora. I know that was difficult for you," the doctor said.

Nora released her breath in a long sigh. Would she and Nicholas finally be able to begin a new life?

She gazed at the doctor. Her heart beat fast as she waited for his decision.

"I knew someday you would tell me the truth about that night in the Fear mansion," he continued. Then the doctor's eyes hardened. "But it is too late, Nora."

"No!" Nora cried as rage rushed through her. "You promised to release me when I realized the truth about that night. A fire destroyed the Fear mansion. A horrible fire. I imagined all the rest."

"It is clear you still believe the Fear family is cursed," the doctor said firmly. "You still need our help. I have arranged for Nicholas to live with a good family until you are ready to be released."

Chapter 4

"Please," Nora wailed. "Please do not take my baby away. He is all I have."

"When you are well, he will be returned to you, I promise," the doctor told her.

Nora backed against the wall. "Your promises are worthless," she spat. "I will not let you take my son."

"You cannot stop me, my dear. You are the patient. I am the doctor. And the family has agreed to pay me a large sum for a male child. I do not want to disappoint them." He signalled to the attendants. They lumbered toward Nora.

She raced across the room and placed Nicholas in his cradle. "I can defend you better if you are not in my arms," she whispered.

She turned and glared at the two men approaching

her. Like the madwoman they claimed she was, she released a wild yell that rose from deep within her soul.

She bared her teeth.

Her nostrils flared and her green eyes narrowed.

Her fingers curled into claws as she lunged at the huge men.

She slashed her fingernails across the neck of the closest man. She felt his skin gather beneath her nails. He yelled as blood flowed down his chest in rivulets. Nora reached for the man's eyes.

The second man grabbed her and yanked her back. She sunk her teeth into his upper arm. Jerking her head back viciously, she ripped out a chunk of his flesh. His agonized scream drowned out the doctor's frantic orders.

The first man knocked Nora to the floor. Breathing heavily, she savored the metallic, salty taste of warm blood on her lips.

"You take one arm, I will take the other," one of the men growled.

Nora scrambled to her feet. Both men lunged at her. She darted to the right. One man caught her arm. He slammed her into the other man. Their hands closed around her arms like iron bands.

She kicked and bucked. She heard laughter. The doctor's laughter. Echoing off the walls. Surrounding her. Suffocating her.

The stale odor of their unwashed bodies filled her nose as she struggled to free herself. She was no match for their strength. She was so tiny. They were so big.

The doctor sauntered over and stood before her. "My dear Nora," he said softly, "continue to fight them, and a slip of their hands could break your neck. Who would care that you died?"

He strolled to the cradle. "Ah, this precious child has made me a rich man."

He leaned down and reached for Nicholas.

"No!" Nora cried in desperation as she fought against her captors. "Keep away from my baby!"

She felt the Fear amulet grow hot against her skin.

The floor shook.

Nora gasped.

The doctor spun around. Eyes wide with fright.

The fire crackled and blazed. The flames grew higher and higher. They reached past the hearth. They climbed the wall. The flames lapped greedily at the ceiling. They grew brighter until all Nora could see was a wall of fire.

A man emerged from the writhing flames.

"Daniel," Nora gasped.

Her husband had come back from the grave.

Nora's legs went weak.

Daniel stared at her. His face serious. His eyes accusing.

"I am sorry," Nora cried. Her voice trembled. "I am so sorry, Daniel. I tried to protect our child—but I could not. Forgive me," she begged.

"Come and join me, Doctor," Daniel rasped. He

reached past Nora and drew the doctor into the raging inferno.

Screaming, the doctor fell to his knees. His eyes bulged. Bulged out farther and farther. Then, with a moist pop, his eyes flew from their sockets and rolled across the floor. They hissed as flames devoured them.

Nora turned her face away from the horrifying sight.

Stunned, the attendants released Nora. She backed toward the cradle. Nicholas would be terrified.

The doctor's agonized shrieks blended with the roaring flames. Nora forced herself to look.

The doctor's skin formed bubbles that burst open to reveal the bone beneath. Bubble, burst, bone. Over and over.

Nora felt a sharp taste hit the back of her throat. She swallowed hard.

Calm down, she ordered herself. You have to be ready to save Nicholas.

The doctor's skin boiled away—until nothing remained but his skeleton.

Daniel dropped the doctor. With a shriek of fury he snatched up one of the attendants—just as the man reached for the doorknob.

The second attendant dashed for the window. Daniel shot flames at him. They covered the attendant like a blanket.

The fire continued to blaze, stretching toward the

corners of the room, painting the ceiling in orange flames.

"Nora!" Daniel shouted.

She jerked her head toward the hearth.

From within the fiery depths of the inferno, Daniel reached out for her.

Chapter 5

Nora felt the heat blasting from Daniel's hands.

"Daniel, no!" she cried. "Don't you recognize me? I am Nora. Your wife. I know you do not want to hurt me."

Strips of skin peeled away from Daniel's face. His burning hands were almost touching her.

Nora could not move. She had to stay in front of the cradle. She had to shield Nicholas.

Nora forced herself to stare into Daniel's glowing white eyes. "Daniel. You must understand. I am Nora. Our son needs me."

"Run, Nora," Daniel rasped.

Nora dashed to the cradle and swept Nicholas up. Then she rushed to the door.

She hesitated a moment and gazed at her husband. The flames retreated to the hearth.

"This is your son," Nora told him, her voice

cracking. "When he grows up he will look just like you."

"Go!" Daniel begged. His face contorted with pain as the flames leapt around him.

"I love you, Daniel," Nora cried.

Daniel released a mournful howl and fell to his knees.

Nora raced from the room and ran down the hallway. The flames followed her. The fire roared around her. The walls became blinding sheets of fire.

The inmates frantically banged on their locked doors. The yells for help were ignored as thick smoke clogged the air.

Hugging Nicholas tightly, Nora rushed down the stairs. The rooms on the next floor were not locked. Patients raced in all directions.

Nora spotted one woman sitting in the middle of the floor, rocking back and forth in a daze. "Fire!" Nora yelled. "Run! The building is on fire! Save yourself!" The woman continued to rock.

Nora began running again.

Faster.

I have to run faster. I have to save Nicholas. I will not let the evil touch him. I will not let the fire burn him.

She darted down the stairs, shoving people aside. Doctors and nurses yelled orders. They did not notice Nora.

A man grabbed the hem of her shift. She heard the material rip as she jerked free and continued to run.

Her eyes stung. The hot air scorched her lungs as she breathed.

Her heart pounded. Her ears rang. Her throat grew dry.

We have to escape, she thought, as she forced her blistered feet down the final flight of stairs. We will escape. We will.

She ran out the front door. Out into the night.

Screeching sirens and clanging bells greeted her. Behind her people screamed, the fire roared, the building began to crumble.

Nora did not pause to catch her breath. She darted across the lawn. The cool grass eased the pain in her feet.

When she reached the safety of the bushes, she crouched and watched the insane asylum burn.

I am free, Nora thought. She could hardly believe it.

What should I do now? Hide. I need a better place to hide. Then I can make plans. Find a way to get out of Shadyside without being seen.

She trailed her fingers along her son's soft cheek. "We must go where no one knows us, Nicholas," she whispered. "We must find a town where no one has ever heard of the Fear family. We must go far, far away."

She looked one last time at the asylum. She could see the window to her room. The bars did not seem so frightening from the outside.

The glass burst out of the window. Like long arms, flames reached out for the nearby trees.

Nora saw Daniel standing at the window. Staring down at them.

"We must go, Nicholas. We must go now. Goodbye, Daniel."

Nora struggled to her feet. Cradling her infant son, she staggered away from the asylum and stumbled toward the unknown.

Chapter 6

Shivering, Nora curled around Nicholas. She felt the warmth from his tiny body as he nestled against her chest. They had taken refuge in the hold of a ship. It held no warmth. It had no fire.

Nora's fingers felt like icicles, frozen and stiff. She was afraid she would wake Nicholas if she touched him with her cold hands.

She knew he was hungry. Just as she was. There had been no time to gather food as they ran from the asylum. No time to think about how they would survive alone, with only each other. She had only cared about escape.

They had traveled through the night. Avoiding the main roads and people, they slowly made their way to the docks in a neighboring town.

With the early-morning fog draped over the land, Nora sneaked aboard the ship. She did not know its destination. She did not care. The ship would take them away. That was enough.

She felt the movement of the boat and heard it scrape against the dock as it headed to sea.

Nora gazed down at her son. Nicholas slept peacefully in a wooden crate lined with some old flour sacks.

Nora's eyelids grew heavy. I must not sleep, she chided herself.

She rubbed her puffy eyes. Her eyes stung when she closed them. They burned when she opened them wide.

I must keep watch, she reminded herself. If I do not, they will come. They move quickly. Even in the darkness, I can feel their tiny beady eyes watching us from the rafters above.

She shuddered. If I close my eyes for a moment, they will attack.

The ship groaned with the motion of the sea. Concentrate on the noises, Nora told herself. Anything to stay awake.

She listened to the footsteps of the sailors overhead as they worked.

The wind whistling across the sea.

The scrabble of tiny feet.

They are moving closer, Nora thought.

Nora peered into the blackness surrounding her. She couldn't see anything.

She felt exhausted. Her body ached.

The skittering of sharp little claws grew louder.

They were coming.

But Nora was too tired. Too tired to worry.

A long, cold, hairless tail brushed along her cheek.

The rats had arrived.

Nora bit back a scream. She forced herself to remain motionless as the rats gathered around her.

I have to maintain my strength. For Nicholas. I must remain strong.

She shot out one hand and snatched one of the rats. It squirmed in her fist, squealing.

Nora broke its neck with a sharp twist, and ripped off its head.

The other rats scattered.

The rat's warm, thick blood oozed across Nora's hand, thawing her icy fingers.

She tilted her head back, fighting against her revulsion. *Have to stay strong for Nicholas. Have to stay strong.*

Nora held the rat over her open mouth and squeezed tightly. Its blood dripped onto her tongue and rolled down her throat.

The door to the cargo hold banged open. Light spilled in through the doorway.

Nora tossed the rat away and wiped the sticky blood from her mouth. She picked Nicholas up and scooted behind a stack of wooden crates.

Footsteps echoed through the hold. Nora watched the light from a lantern bounce across the floor and walls.

The light moved closer and closer. The footsteps grew louder.

Nora held her breath.

Then the light moved away.

All grew still. Silent.

Where is the man? she wondered. Is he going to leave?

Nora held her breath. Please leave! she thought. Please go away and leave us in peace.

Nora strained to hear something that would give away the man's location. But she heard nothing. Not even the scurrying of the rats.

Nora's heart thudded. She waited. Where is the man? Where is he?

Cautiously, she inched forward and peered around the wooden crates.

Large, rough hands grabbed her and yanked her to her feet.

"I knew I heard more than rats moving around down here," the man cried.

Nora struggled to break free.

"Do you know what we do with stowaways?" he demanded. Nora shook her head. "We throw them to the sharks!"

The man narrowed his eyes and studied her. Nora's thoughts raced. What is he going to do to me? I have to keep him away from Nicholas.

"Give me that necklace you are wearing and I will not tell anyone you are here," the man ordered.

"But it was a gift from—"

"I want it," he snarled. "And one way or another, I will have it. You can give it to me or I will take it."

He wrapped his fingers around the silver chain.

"No!" Nora shrieked. The amulet grew warm against her skin.

"I want it!" he growled. He twisted the chain and gave it a hard jerk.

The chain tightened around her neck and dug into her throat. She gasped for air. She struggled to squeeze her fingers underneath the chain. Air. She needed air.

Darkness surrounded her. Her hands fell limply to her sides.

Nicholas. Who would take care of Nicholas?

From far away Nora heard the man utter a shrill scream of agony. The pressure around her throat eased.

Damp, salty air rushed into her lungs. She forced her eyes open and looked at the man. If she had had the strength, she would have screamed.

Rats swarmed over the man. They dropped on him from the rafters. They scurried up his pant legs. They crawled down the collar of his shirt.

More rats jumped from the crates, fighting for a place on his twisting and thrashing body. The rats scratched and chewed until Nora could see pieces of the man's white bones.

Nora's stomach twisted as she watched the rats. They ripped at the man with their claws and their sharp yellow teeth. One rat yanked away a chunk of the man's earlobe. One pulled off a tiny piece of his eyelid.

The man howled in agony—and one of the rats leapt into his mouth.

The man fell to the floor. He curled himself into a tight ball. Nora heard him whimpering.

Whimpering as the rats fed on his flesh.

What if they are still hungry when they have finished? Nora thought.

She positioned herself in front of Nicholas's makeshift cradle and stared at the rats.

They would have to get through her before they touched her baby.

Chapter 7

Heavy footsteps pounded down the stairs.

The door crashed open and men poured in. Sailors, shipmen, workers.

What will they do if they find me? Nora slowly backed into the corner.

Lifting their lanterns, the men stared in mute horror as the black rats swarmed over their shipmate. Pools of dark blood glistened around him.

One of the men snatched up a crate and hurled it at the rats. A few ran off. The rest kept feeding.

Nora's stomach cramped when she caught sight of the spongy gray brain matter spilling from the man's head.

"There is no saving him," one of the sailors muttered.

Nicholas gave a little whimper.

Please do not cry now, Nora begged silently. Please. Not until they are gone—and we are safe again.

She jiggled Nicholas up and down. He liked that. It usually made him stop crying.

Nora shifted from one foot to the other as she tried to keep the baby quiet. One of her feet came down on a piece of wood.

It snapped with a *crack.*

"Look!" A man pointed at Nora. A shiver raced through her as all the men turned and stared at her.

"The rats left her alone," another man whispered hoarsely.

"She must possess some dark magic," someone called. The men murmured in agreement.

"No!" Nora cried. "I have no magic. You must believe me."

One man edged nearer. He had straw-colored hair and freckles.

"I am Tim." He puffed out his chest. "First mate." He glanced at the bloody body on the floor. Still. So still. "This is not a safe place for a woman and a baby. Follow me."

Some of the men muttered in protest. Tim pushed his way through the crowd. Nora was careful to stay close behind him.

They trudged up the stairs. The other men fell in behind them. Nora noticed that none of them came too close to her. They are afraid of me, she realized. Afraid, but angry, too.

"This way," Tim urged. When Tim reached the end

of the corridor, he pushed open the last door. "In here, missy."

Nora stepped inside the small room. Beds were stacked one on top of another along two walls. Large wooden trunks lined another wall. Above the trunks, pegs in the wall held yellow rain slickers.

Tim opened a wooden trunk. He took out the clothes and tossed them into a corner. Then he took a blanket from the bed and dropped it into the trunk. "You can put the baby in here," he said gruffly.

Nora placed Nicholas in the trunk. She wrapped the blanket around him. Grateful, she started to thank Tim. But his eyes were hard and cold.

"You are not to leave this room," he commanded. "I will have to discuss your presence with the captain."

"Shouldn't I talk to the captain?" Nora asked.

Tim shook his head. "A woman on board a cargo ship is bad luck. He won't like this. He won't like it at all."

He shut the door firmly behind him, and Nora heard a key turn in the lock.

Nora sank down on the floor beside the trunk. I am a prisoner again, she realized. She stroked Nicholas's back gently. But at least there are no rats here. And we have light.

Now if they will just bring us some food.

The ship lurched. Waves crashed down on it.

She grabbed the edge of the trunk and held on tightly. She crooned to the baby as the ship pitched back and forth.

"It is a storm, Nicholas," she said. "That is all. A storm. The men are used to storms at sea. They know what to do."

Nora heard a man yelling orders. She thought he sounded scared.

She heard footsteps racing back and forth above her.

The ship pitched more violently. Nora braced herself against one wall, fighting to keep Nicholas's trunk steady.

What is happening to us? Nora wondered. *What is happening to us now?*

"One minute the sea is calm—now this," Nora heard a man yell. "It is not natural."

"It is that woman!" another man yelled. "She has dark powers!"

The ship plunged. Nora was thrown against the door of her room. Nicholas's trunk slammed into her.

Nicholas squealed in fright. Nora tried to comfort him. But her voice shook as she whispered to him, and her heart thudded against her ribs.

Nora heard footsteps racing down the corridor. "She brought this down on us!" a man shouted from outside the door.

"Yes!" another man shouted. "She controlled those rats. She had them kill Frank. She will kill us all if we let her."

"I did not kill your friend," Nora called through the door. "Please believe me!"

"Why should we believe her?" one of the men growled.

Nora pulled Nicholas's trunk as far away from the door as she could. "I will keep you safe," she promised him. "Do not worry. Mama will keep you safe."

"Throw her overboard!" someone yelled.

Nora returned to the door and stood waiting for the men.

The key turned in the lock. The door flew open.

A man charged in and grabbed her by the waist. Nora fought wildly, scratching and kicking.

The man swore and hoisted her over one of his shoulders.

"Let me go!" Nora screamed. She twisted back and forth. Trying to break free. "I have to stay with my baby!"

The big man tightened his grip and hauled her out of the room and up some narrow stairs.

He shoved open the door leading to the deck. The wind caught it and tore it from its hinges. Nora screamed.

The rain pelted Nora as the man carried her outside. The wind stung her face. Waves rushed over the railing each time the ship lurched.

Nora could not stop shaking. How could she convince these men she was innocent?

The man stalked toward the railing. "Throw her over! Throw her over!" the other men chanted.

The man slid Nora off his shoulder. Her unsteady feet hit the deck. "Stop the storm!" the man yelled.

Nora staggered in the wind. He grabbed her arm, his fingers digging into her tender skin.

"Stop the storm!" he yelled again.

Nora shook her head. "I cannot. You have to let me go back to my baby. Please!"

The sailors howled in fury. They rushed forward and hoisted her into the air.

She struggled as they carried her to the rail. "Stop! I have no magic!" Nora screamed. "I have no power over the storm!"

"Throw her overboard!" someone yelled into the wind.

The men lifted her higher.

They swung her over the railing.

The ocean churned beneath her.

Chapter 8

The ship lurched.

The men stumbled backward—away from the railing.

They released Nora. She felt herself falling.

Nora landed on the deck. Pain burst through her chest as the air was knocked out of her.

A powerful wave crashed over the railing. Nora heard men scream as the wave pulled them over. Gasping for breath, she struggled to her knees.

I must get to Nicholas. This ship cannot survive this storm. It will sink. It will sink to the bottom of the ocean. I cannot let it take Nicholas with it.

Nora felt the Fear amulet grow warm against her chest. She wrapped her fingers around it.

The bow of the ship lurched into the air. Straight up. Nora grabbed onto some rigging and wrapped it around her hands.

Men slid past her, clawing at the deck. They screamed in terror as they fell into the sea.

The bow plunged back into the water. Nora shook free of the rigging. She crawled to the stairs and tumbled halfway down.

Nora heard the wind scream. Water poured down the stairs. She hauled herself to her feet and braced a hand against the wall to keep her balance.

The amulet began to glow. Its strange blue light helped Nora find her way. When she reached the bottom of the stairs, icy water swirled above her ankles. "Nicholas!" she cried. "I'm coming!"

She struggled down the hallway and threw open the last door. The trunk had not been moved. And she could see Nicholas's fists waving in the air.

"I am here!" she cried, lunging for the trunk.

A strong hand landed on her shoulder and stopped her.

Nora spun around. No one could keep her from Nicholas. No one.

"You must die!" the sailor yelled.

"No!" Nora shrieked.

She had to save Nicholas. She had to save her baby.

Chapter 9

She grabbed the man's shirt.

She felt power rush through her body. She felt strong enough to fight every man on the ship—if that is what it took to save her son.

She lifted the man into the air. And hurled him against the wall with all her might.

Thunk!

A wooden clothes-peg burst through his chest.

Hot, sticky blood sprayed across Nora's face.

The man howled in agony as he hung suspended from the peg.

"Look what she did to Samuel," someone screamed.

Nora turned toward the voice.

Three men stared back at her.

"She *is* evil!" one of the men declared. "Pure evil."

"That's right! I am evil!" Nora screamed. "Stay back! Stay back or I will kill you as well."

She stroked the amulet. Its heat flowed through her fingers.

The men hesitated. Nora could tell they were frightened. Frightened and angry.

"I have the power. I will use it. Run from me while you can!" She meant every word of her threat. She would kill them. She would kill them all to protect Nicholas.

Nora rushed at the men. "Run while you can!"

The men scrambled over one another as they bolted from the room.

Crack!

Nora heard the sharp sound above the storm.

Water began seeping through the walls of the cabin. The sides of the ship are splintering, Nora realized.

She rushed to Nicholas. The trunk was made of solid wood, but would it float? Or sink to the bottom of the sea?

She spotted a coiled rope on the floor. She snatched it up and tied one end securely around her small waist. She kissed the tips of her fingers, then pressed her fingers to her son's cheek. "Keep safe."

She closed the lid on the trunk and ran her hand over the finely polished wood grain. "Keep safe, my baby."

The ship lurched and rolled. Water poured into the room faster and faster.

Nora wrapped the rope securely around the trunk.

Over and under. Knot. Knot. Around. Another knot. Beneath and over. Another knot.

The cold seawater circled her calves. The chest rose slowly with the rising level of water in the cabin. Nora tied another knot.

"We will be all right, Nicholas," Nora murmured as the water crept higher and higher.

The wooden planks of the ship creaked and moaned.

Nora watched in horror as the planks buckled. They are not going to hold, she realized.

The planks caved in. A huge wave crashed down on Nora. It filled the cabin with water.

The icy saltwater surrounded her. It burned her mouth and nose. It stung her eyes.

Nora struggled to the hole in the cabin wall. She had to get out. She needed air. Her lungs burned.

She pulled herself through the hole, tugging Nicholas's trunk behind her.

Then she swam as hard as she could. Up, up, up. She had to reach the surface.

The trunk bumped into her side, into her shoulder, against her head. Pain shot through her. Dots of light burst before her eyes.

Nora shot up to the surface. She sucked in a huge gulp of air.

The gale lashed at her unmercifully. It flung the trunk away from her—but the rope held.

Nora coughed and gagged. Her water-soaked clothes weighed her down.

She pulled the trunk back to her and clung to it. It

helped her stay afloat as the waves crashed around her.

Nora heard the men scream as they were thrown into the sea. They struggled to keep their heads above the churning water.

As Nora watched, the ship slowly sank beneath the water. Down, down, down.

Then the wind stopped.

The sea calmed.

The screams stopped.

What happened to the men? Nora thought. She searched the ocean around her for survivors.

But the dark waters had become as still as a glass mirror.

Nicholas's trunk bobbed up and down. Nothing else stirred.

Not one of the men lived.

A deadly peace spread its cloak over them.

Nora felt exhausted. Every muscle and bone in her body ached.

I just want to sleep, she thought to herself. But I must not. I have to save Nicholas. I have to find the shore. I have to find safety.

She slipped off the trunk and into the cold water. With great effort, she began swimming, pulling the trunk behind her.

She tasted blood on her lips. Blood and salt. She did not know if the salt came from the water surrounding her . . . or from her own tears.

Nora's arms grew heavy. She forced them over her head again and again.

Her legs began to cramp, but she continued to kick. How much farther? Where is the land?

Nora heard a mighty roar. She stopped swimming and clung to the trunk. She scanned the water.

Her eyes widened. Dark clouds circled over the sea. Lightning lit the sky.

The waves stirred, rising up from the depths of the ocean.

The storm had returned.

She scrambled onto the trunk. And waited.

Waited for death to claim her.

Roaring, the storm advanced. Huge waves tossed the trunk up and down. The ropes dug into Nora's fingers as she hung on.

She was at the mercy of the storm.

And it had no mercy.

Chapter 10

Nora felt the fine spray mist her face. She was tired, so terribly tired. She only wanted to sleep.

Painfully, slowly, Nora opened her eyes.

She was no longer clinging to the trunk. She lay sprawled upon the ground. Sand stuck to her face and her bare legs.

She bolted upright.

Nicholas! Where was Nicholas?

Nora's eyes darted around the beach. She spotted the trunk—and gasped.

The trunk had smashed into a huge rock. The lid was open.

Was Nicholas still inside? Was he hurt?

Nora scrambled to her feet and ran toward the trunk. She slipped on the wet sand and fell to her knees.

She forced herself to her feet and staggered forward. With dread filling her heart, she gazed into the trunk.

Nicholas rested there.

Still.

So very still.

"Nicholas?" she whispered in a raspy voice.

He did not move.

Seagulls flew overhead, but even their screeching did not wake him.

He is dead, Nora thought dully. Nicholas is dead.

Tears welled in her eyes. She reached out and touched her baby's cheek. "Nicholas?"

He scrunched his face and released a long wail. He was alive!

Nora laughed, lifted him out of the chest, and held him close.

The warm breeze caressed her face as she stood on the sandy shore. "We are safe, Nicholas. Safe."

Nora walked into the ocean until it lapped around her knees. She stared at the crystal-blue water that stretched into eternity. "We will start a new life together," she promised Nicholas.

He reached up with one tiny hand and grabbed the chain of her amulet. The chain snapped. The amulet fell to the ground.

Nora picked it up and studied it. She turned it over and read the inscription: DOMINATIO PER MALUM.

"Power through evil," Nora whispered. "Your father gave this to me as a symbol of his love, Nicholas. The amulet was special to him, because it had been in his family for a long time."

Nora sighed. "Your father's family had power and money. But they paid a heavy price. They let evil into their lives, and it destroyed them."

Nora stared down into the ocean for a long moment. "I do not want that evil to be a part of your life, Nicholas. I do not want you to suffer the same fate your father did."

The amulet felt heavy in her hand. Heavy and warm.

Nora brought her arm back and flung it into the calm sea.

Relief swept through her. She hugged Nicholas. "Now the Fear evil cannot touch you."

Nora stared down into her baby's face. "We are going to start a new life—with new names. From now on, we will be known as Nora and Nicholas Storm."

PART TWO

Chapter 11

Shadow Cove 1919

Nicholas Storm hated being a fisherman.

He hated the feel of slimy fish. The taste of salt on his lips. The odor of brine that filled his nostrils.

As he trudged home, he carried the stink of fish with him. No matter how often he bathed or how hard he scrubbed, the stench clung to his skin. He hated it.

He hated everything in his life. Everything.

Everything but Rosalyn.

Rosalyn was different. She did not belong to Shadow Cove. Rosalyn came from Spain.

Nicholas loved her long black hair and dark brown eyes. And the tiny gold studs she wore in her pierced ears.

None of the other girls in Shadow Cove had pierced ears. None of the other girls were anything like Rosalyn.

The other girls in their town only wanted to get

married and settle down. Have babies. And eat the fish their husbands caught.

Rosalyn wanted more. And so did Nicholas. They wanted to get married and leave Shadow Cove together.

But Rosalyn's father would never give them permission to wed. He had strict requirements for the man who would marry his daughter—the man had to be rich and powerful. As rich and powerful as Rosalyn's father.

Rosalyn had been forbidden even to speak to Nicholas. They always had to meet in secret.

Nicholas promised himself he would make Rosalyn's father accept him someday. No matter what it took. And then he and Rosalyn *would* get married.

Nicholas strode up to the house he shared with his mother. The salt air had faded the warped, weather-beaten boards to a dull gray.

Nicholas pushed open the door and stepped into the kitchen. He came to an abrupt halt.

The house stood dark and silent. Too silent.

Flies buzzed around the eggs he had left on his plate at breakfast. "Mother!" he called, wondering why she had not washed the dishes.

A crab skittered sideways across the wooden floor.

Slowly Nicholas walked through the kitchen into the front room. Empty.

Nicholas heard a low groan. He ran down the hallway and barged into his mother's room. He found his mother curled into a ball on the floor.

She did not move as Nicholas rushed over to her.

Her face was as white as the shells that washed up on the beach. Her eyes were closed.

He knelt beside her and took her hand. It felt as cold as ice. "Mother?" he whispered hoarsely. The stench of death surrounded her.

Nicholas rubbed his mother's hand with both of his. Her hand felt cold. Too cold. "Mother, what is wrong?" he cried. "Are you ill?"

Nora struggled to open her eyes. She stared up at him. "Daniel?" she rasped.

Relief washed through Nicholas. "No, Mother. It is Nicholas."

Nora smiled wistfully. "You look so like your father."

"So you have often said," Nicholas replied. "Now tell me what happened," he urged.

"My heart . . ." Her words trailed off.

He scooped his mother up in his arms. Light. She felt so light.

When did she begin to look so old? he wondered as he stared down at her. His mother had the appearance of a woman twice her age. Her once bright green eyes were dull. Her once brown hair now gray.

Grief tightened around his heart as he gently lowered her to her bed. He picked up the coverlet from the floor and wrapped it around her.

His mother had worked so hard to support them. As soon as he was old enough, Nicholas had gotten a job on one of the fishing boats. But for years his mother had taken care of him all alone.

He remembered the hours his mother had spent

sewing, and washing clothes, and mending fishnets to earn enough money for them to eat and keep their little house.

Nicholas always promised himself that when he made his fortune, he would give his mother everything she wanted. She would never have to work another day.

Nicholas sat down next to his mother. Time was slipping away from him, like sand through his fingers. He realized he would never be able to give his mother the things she deserved.

"Nicholas. I have something to tell you," his mother said, her voice weak. "I wanted to protect you, but . . ."

Protect me from what? Nicholas thought. A shiver ran through him.

Nora swallowed. "You need to know the truth about your family. I will not always be here to protect you."

Nicholas felt his throat tighten. He wanted to tell his mother that she would be around to protect him for years and years. But he knew it was a lie.

Seagulls screeched in the distance. Wind whipped through the house, shaking the doors and windows.

His mother looked deeply into his eyes. Her expression so intense it almost frightened Nicholas.

"Your father . . . your father . . ." she began.

"Tell me," Nicholas begged. "Tell me."

He had waited so long to hear about his father. His mother had never spoken of him—except to say

Nicholas looked just like his father. Now he would finally learn the truth.

"Your father left you a legacy . . ." Nora told him. She gasped for breath. "A legacy of . . ."

Her body spasmed. Nicholas heard a rattling sound deep in his mother's chest.

The death rattle.

Her hands released their grip.

She fell back on the bed. Her eyes stared blankly up at Nicholas.

She is dead, Nicholas thought. My mother is dead.

Chapter 12

Nicholas heard his mother's words over and over as he stood beside her grave. *I wanted to protect you . . . Your father left you a legacy . . .*

Would he ever understand? Would he ever learn what she wanted to protect him from?

Would he ever have the legacy his father wanted to give him?

Nicholas shivered in the cold wind. He wished Rosalyn were here. He needed to talk to her. She would help him figure things out.

He knew Rosalyn had wanted to be with him at the funeral. But her father would not allow it.

If I already had my legacy, I bet Rosalyn's father would change his mind about me. Rosalyn and I could be married right away.

When the sun set, Nicholas walked away from his

mother's grave. He wandered down to the beach and stared at the vast ocean spread before him. The full moon reflected off the water.

Nicholas did not want to go home. The little house would feel too empty without his mother there. Tears stung Nicholas's eyes.

He did not want to cry. He strode down the beach. Moving faster and faster. Then breaking into a run.

He ran until his heart pounded painfully and his lungs burned. Ran until he heard someone call his name.

Rosalyn!

The blue silk of her dress billowed as she raced toward him. The blue stones of her favorite necklace captured the moonbeams.

Rosalyn threw herself into his arms. Nicholas held her tight. So tight. He never wanted to let her go.

He rested his cheek on her head. Her long black hair smelled like the rose perfume she always wore. And it felt so soft.

With a sigh, Rosalyn stepped back and lifted her gaze to his. Her dark eyes held a serious expression.

Nicholas bent down and kissed her tenderly. Her full lips felt soft and welcoming. Then he cradled her face in his hands. "Rosalyn, what is wrong?" he asked quietly.

"You must leave," Rosalyn blurted out. She pressed her face against his chest. He felt her trembling against him. "You must leave Shadow Cove right away."

"Why?"

She looked up at him, tears filling her eyes. "Tonight, my father told me that he is planning to arrange a marriage for me. A marriage to a wealthy man, a man who can take care of me. I was so upset. Without thinking, I told him I love you."

Nicholas gritted his teeth. "Was he furious?"

She nodded. "He vowed he would kill you before he allowed us to marry." She wrapped her fingers around his arm. "You must leave. My father does not make threats he will not carry out."

"There is something I have to tell you. Something that might make your father change his mind about me," Nicholas said. "Before she died, my mother told me my father had left me a legacy."

"Did she tell you who your father was?" Rosalyn asked.

Nicholas shook his head. "But I will find out. I have to."

Rosalyn looked doubtful.

Nicholas rushed on. "Even if I do not, I will find a way to make my fortune. I plan to leave Shadow Cove tomorrow. When I have enough money to convince your father to give us his blessing, I will come home. And then we will be married. Promise me you will not let your father force you to marry anyone else."

Tears glistened on her face. "When you return, I will marry you," she told him. "I promise I will never marry another. No matter what my father does."

"I will hold you to that promise," he said.

She gave him a shaky smile. "I must go before my father discovers I am gone."

"I will come back for you, Rosalyn," Nicholas promised again. He wrapped his arms around her and kissed her. He would miss her so much.

Rosalyn eased out of his embrace. "Please take care."

"I will." Nicholas's throat tightened as he watched her race away from him. When she disappeared from his sight, he turned and headed toward his empty house.

Dark clouds passed before the moon, hiding the faint light. Nicholas hurried up the beach and back to the dirt road. He heard a sound behind him—like a twig snapping. He twisted his head and scanned the road. Empty.

He slowed down, but kept moving. Cautiously, he turned his head slightly and glanced behind him. Out of the corner of his eye, he spotted a shadow move.

Is someone following me?

Nicholas shot another quick look behind him. A man ducked back into the shadows.

Had Rosalyn's father sent someone after him already?

Nicholas kept walking. He did not want the man to know he had been seen.

When Nicholas reached a large elm tree, he ducked behind it. He wanted to get a better look at the man.

Nicholas peered through the branches.

The road stood empty.

Where did he go?

Nicholas heard a shuffling sound behind him. He spun around.

The man stood in front of him.

"It cannot be!" Nicholas cried.

The man looked just like him.

Chapter 13

"Who are you?" Nicholas demanded. He hoped the man could not see him trembling.

How could the man look exactly like him?

The man stared back at Nicholas in silence, his face blank.

Nicholas felt the hair on the back of his neck stand up. "Who are you?" he shouted again.

His eyes darted over the young man. Same dark brown eyes as mine, Nicholas thought frantically. Same straight brown hair. Same height.

Calm down, Nicholas ordered himself. Calm down. It is only a strange coincidence. Brown hair is not uncommon. Brown eyes are not . . .

No. That does not explain it, Nicholas thought. He does not look like me. He *is* me.

"What do you want? What are you?" Nicholas cried.

The other man opened and closed his mouth. But no sound came out.

"Can't you speak?" he barked.

The man stared at Nicholas pleadingly.

He opened his mouth again. "Shadyside!" he croaked.

The man's face contorted. As though speech were agonizing to him.

The man began to fade.

"I don't understand," Nicholas cried. "What did you come to tell me?" Nicholas could hardly see the man now.

"Shadyside," the man shrieked.

Then he was gone.

Chapter 14

"One ticket to Shadyside," Nicholas said.

He anxiously watched the man behind the counter in the train station. Nicholas did not know if a place called Shadyside even existed. But the man gave him a curt nod, took his money, and handed him a ticket.

Nicholas had been unable to sleep the night before. He kept thinking about his strange vision.

Then he knew what he had to do. At dawn he packed his few possessions and made the long walk to the train station.

He did not know what he would find in Shadyside. But he had to start his search for his father's legacy somewhere. Perhaps the vision had been sent to guide him.

Nicholas paced up and down the platform. He could not wait to leave and find out what awaited him in Shadyside.

Nicholas straightened the lapels of his new brown suit. He had bought it on the way to the train station. He was off to seek his fortune. He did not want to look like a poor fisherman.

His mind on his journey, Nicholas bumped into a woman in a straw hat. She stood hunched over, a shawl wrapped around her shoulders.

"Excuse me, ma'am," Nicholas said.

The woman glanced up. Her brown eyes held his.

"Rosalyn!" he cried in surprise.

He grabbed her arm and led her away from the few passengers waiting to board the train.

"What are you doing here?" he asked when they were safely out of sight.

"I wanted to see you one more time," she explained. "So I decided to come to the train station. I knew I would find you!"

He squeezed her hand. "I am glad you did," he told her. "I have something to tell you. When I was walking home last night, I had a vision."

Rosalyn gave a little gasp. "What happened?"

"It is difficult to explain," Nicholas told her. "It was a vision of myself. This vision of me spoke only one word—Shadyside."

Nicholas pulled out his ticket and showed it to her. "I did not even know if such a place existed. But it does. So that is where I will begin my search for my father's legacy."

Rosalyn shivered. "I do not like the idea of you following this vision," she said. "You do not know if it came from good or evil—even though it took your form."

"I know it is a strange thing to do," Nicholas admitted. "But I feel it is my . . . my destiny."

Rosalyn nodded. "I understand. Good luck, Nicholas. Stay well. I will count the minutes until you return. But I must go. My father will be furious if he finds out I saw you."

Rosalyn thrust a small package into his hands. "Here. I want you to take more than my love with you."

She wrapped her arms around his neck and kissed him. Nicholas held her tight and breathed in the scent of roses that always clung to her.

Then she pulled her shawl over her head, glanced around, and scurried away. Nicholas slipped the package into the pocket of his jacket. He heard a whistle blow and spotted the train far down the tracks.

He could not wait to begin his journey. Faster, he silently urged the train. Faster, faster. Finally it pulled into the station, the brakes squealing.

Nicholas climbed aboard and made his way to a padded seat next to a window. He had never been on a train before. He had never been anywhere outside Shadow Cove.

The train whistle blew and black smoke raced past the window.

The train lurched forward.

Nicholas pressed his forehead against the window. *When I return to Shadow Cove, no one will recognize* me, he thought. No one will believe I am Nicholas Storm, the boy who always stank of fish.

Nicholas reached into his pocket for a peppermint and felt Rosalyn's package. He had forgotten all about it. He unfolded the note and read the words she had written in her beautiful flowing script:

Dearest Nicholas,

When I was a child, I often walked along the shore. One evening as the sun began to set, I saw something shining just below the sand. A gift from the sea.

It is my most precious possession. And it has always brought me good luck. I was wearing it the day I met you!

I want you to take it with you on your journey. I know it will bring you safely back to me.

Love always, Rosalyn

He pulled on the string tied around the package. It fell free and the brown paper opened to reveal Rosalyn's gift.

Rosalyn's favorite necklace. He had seen her wear it so often. He held it tightly in his hand. It felt warm to his touch. Warm from her skin, he thought, although he knew that was impossible.

Nicholas opened his hand and studied the necklace. It was unusual. The flat silver disk held a circle of sparkling blue stones. The disk was bigger than the ornaments on most necklaces. It is more like an amulet, Nicholas thought.

Three claws attached the amulet to the chain. "Strange decoration," Nicholas muttered. He ran his thumb over the silver claws.

Oww! A drop of blood fell from his thumb into the center of the amulet. Those things are sharp, Nicholas thought.

He started to shove the amulet back into his pocket. Then he caught sight of an inscription on the back.

These are Latin words, he realized. He struggled to remember enough Latin to translate them.

"Per." That was easy. "Per" meant "through."

"Dominatio," he whispered to himself. "Dominatio." Oh, right. "Dominatio" is like "dominate." It means "power."

Now "malum." Think. What does malum mean?

Evil.

Nicholas's fingers tightened around the amulet as the meaning of the inscription came to him.

DOMINATIO PER MALUM.

POWER THROUGH EVIL.

PART THREE

Chapter 15

The Village of Shadyside
1919

A storm was brewing.

Nicholas could feel it in the wind as he climbed onto the narrow concrete platform of the Shadyside train station. He could smell it in the air.

Lightning flashed in the darkening sky. It outlined part of a large mansion looming in the distance.

Nicholas had planned to find a room in a hotel and explore Shadyside the next day. Instead he picked up his suitcase and wandered through the town square and down the tree-lined main street.

He passed the barber shop, its peppermint-striped pole out front. A young marine was getting a shave inside. Just back from the war, Nicholas thought. And he is not much older than I am.

He peered through the window of the general store. The shelves were crammed with tools, dishes, bolts of cloth, bags of flour, jars of candy—everything the townspeople might want. Nicholas thought about going inside for a cold drink, but decided to continue on.

He felt as if the mansion were a magnet, drawing him nearer. Pulling him closer and closer. He did not want to stop for anything until he reached it.

Nicholas passed the telegraph office and the newspaper office. He gave the wooden Indian outside the tobacco shop a pat on the shoulder as he went by. And he whistled in appreciation when he spotted the shiny new Mercer Runabout parked in front of the bank.

Someday I will have an auto such as that, Nicholas promised himself.

Nicholas walked faster and faster. He had to see that mansion. He turned off the main street and hurried down a row of small houses. Almost every one had a vegetable garden.

At last Nicholas found the street leading to the mansion—Fear Street. Strange name. Who would want to live on a street with such a name?

A stretch of the winding street had been paved. The rest had not. Someone must have had plans for this land, Nicholas realized. But it appears that they abandoned their project long ago.

Nicholas heard thunder rumble in the distance. He knew he should turn back. Find a place to spend the night. But he needed to see that mansion.

Nicholas rushed down the winding road until he reached the iron gate leading to the mansion. He pushed the gate open, and the hinges squealed.

Thorns snagged the pants of his new brown suit as

he struggled up the overgrown driveway. He did not care.

Nicholas's heart beat faster and faster as he approached the house. I belong here, he thought suddenly. I belong here.

He stopped in front of the mansion. It towered over him. It was huge. Nicholas could not imagine living there. The first floor alone would hold five or six cottages such as the one he and his mother had shared.

Most of the enormous house had been destroyed. A fire, Nicholas decided. A big one. I bet people could see it all over town.

Nicholas tried to imagine the mansion as it once was. A vision popped into his head. The house freshly painted. The shutters open. Light pouring from the windows. The gardens and hedges well cared for.

Another roll of thunder sounded in the distance. I am going to get caught in the rain, Nicholas thought.

But he could not head back to town now.

This place calls to me, Nicholas thought. But why? For what purpose? For good . . . or evil? The hair on his arms stood up.

Nicholas climbed up the porch steps, the wood creaking beneath his feet. He hesitated, then slipped inside the charred remains of the huge house.

His mouth grew dry, and he swallowed hard as he put down his suitcase. I know this room. I know what it looked like before the fire. I know what I will find in every room of this mansion.

Had he seen the house in a dream? A nightmare? What was happening to him?

A dim gray light shone into the room. Nicholas looked up. The fire had burned a hole from the ground floor up through the roof of the mansion. Leaving only a burnt-out shell.

The smell of burning wood still filled the room. Did people die in the fire? he wondered.

"Fire," he heard a voice whisper behind him. He spun around.

But no one stood there.

It is only the wind, he thought. A memory flashed through his mind. His mother saying those same words to him, comforting him. Only the wind.

The wind swirled around him. *"Fire. Fire. Fire."*

Nicholas forced himself to stand still and listen to the whispering voices. He could only understand a few of the words.

"Curse."

He closed his eyes and listened harder.

"Fear."

"Evil."

Evil. Fear. Curse. Nicholas's eyes snapped open. Were the voices trying to warn him? Was he in danger?

"Who are you?" he cried. "Who calls to me?"

The smell of burning flesh filled his nostrils. His eyes stung and itched.

"Answer me," he pleaded.

The ragged drapes in front of one charred window

frame fluttered. Nicholas sucked his breath in with a hiss.

A large scorch mark covered the drapes. A scorch mark in the shape of a human body.

Nicholas edged closer to the drapes. The scorch mark grew darker. Thicker. It bulged out, straining away from the fabric.

Nicholas heard a tearing sound. The body is ripping through the drapes! he thought. It is coming for me!

Nicholas backed away, his heartbeat pounding in his ears. And the body disappeared.

He caught sight of a figure deep in the shadows in the far corner of the room. An old man in a wheelchair. Watching him.

"Who are you?" Nicholas demanded. "Why didn't you let me know you were there?"

The old man did not answer.

Nicholas could not see the man's expression. The shadows concealed everything but the shape of his body.

Nicholas rushed over. But the old man disappeared before Nicholas could reach him.

I have to get out of here, Nicholas thought. Now. Before I go mad.

He turned toward the front of the house.

The dark shape of a woman appeared there. Blocking his exit. He noticed the silhouette of a knife held high in the woman's hand.

Go on, Nicholas ordered himself. She cannot hurt you. She is like the others. She will disappear.

Nicholas forced himself to cross the room, heading toward the woman.

He felt his legs trembling. He had seen and heard too much in this strange old house.

Almost there, Nicholas thought. All I have to do is step around the woman and I will be out of this cursed mansion.

Nicholas took a deep breath and strode forward.

Lightning flashed across the sky and glinted off the steel knife in the woman's hand.

Steel!

The woman shrieked. She raised the knife higher, then thrust it down at Nicholas's chest.

Chapter 16

Nicholas saw the steel of the knife shine as it slashed toward him.

He heard the material of his shirt rip.

He felt the sharp, cold edge of the knife against his skin.

Then Nicholas caught the woman's wrist. He jerked her arm back before she could plunge the knife into him.

"You are dead, Daniel Fear!" the woman screamed. "You must stay dead!"

She raked the fingernails of her free hand across Nicholas's face. He felt blood trickle down his cheek.

Cursing, Nicholas grabbed the woman's other hand. He held both of her wrists tightly.

She shrieked, jerking back and forth, frantically trying to free herself. "You and your evil must stay dead!" she yelled again.

Thunder crashed. Raindrops began to fall through the open roof.

Nicholas fought to keep his grip as his hands slid across the woman's wet skin.

A flash of lightning illuminated the woman. Her face was contorted with rage. Her eyes bulged. Her mouth stretched open in a long, high-pitched cry.

Nicholas squeezed the woman's right wrist until the knife fell from her grip. It clattered to the floor.

He flung the woman away from him and snatched the knife from the floor. Breathing heavily, Nicholas backed up, ready to defend himself again.

The woman sank to the floor. She covered her face and began to cry. "Take me with you, Daniel Fear. Take me to the land of the dead. Take me to the place where you live as a ghost so I may again be with my love."

Nicholas stared down at the weeping woman. She is mad. What is she raving about? Why is she here? The house is not fit to live in.

The woman began to shake. She curled her body into a ball, still hiding her face.

She is terrified of me, Nicholas realized. He slid the knife across the room and knelt beside the woman. "I am sorry I frightened you. I am not Daniel Fear. My name is Nicholas Storm."

The woman snapped her head up, a wild look in her eyes. "Liar. I would know you anywhere. If you are not Daniel Fear, you are his ghost."

"Where do you live?" Nicholas asked, careful to

keep his voice low. He did not want to alarm her again. "Let me take you home. You cannot stay out in this rain."

"I live here," the woman answered. She scrambled to her feet and motioned for Nicholas to follow her.

The woman scurried. She led him to a room Nicholas thought had once been the pantry.

Rows of shelves had survived the fire. They held a few pieces of clothing, an old rag doll, some dried flowers, and a little food. An old mattress and threadbare blanket filled one corner. Several candles gave the only light.

"Did the Fear family live here?" Nicholas asked. Perhaps the strange woman could give him some idea why he felt so drawn to the mansion.

"Of course they did. You know that, Daniel Fear," the woman answered.

Nicholas did not bother to correct her. She could call him Daniel if that would help him get the information he needed.

"Your grandparents lived here," the woman continued. "Simon and Angelica Fear. They died here, too. Just like you. Everyone died, and they must stay dead. Even you must stay dead. And my love. My Charles."

"Who is Charles?" Nicholas asked. He had to keep her talking.

The woman reached out and squeezed his hand. "Charles. Remember, he used to help out when your grandparents gave parties. He was my fiancé. He died here the night of the fire."

"Were you here that night?"

"No," she answered, her voice cracking. "I planned to help out in the kitchen, but I got sick that night. I had to stay home."

"Do you know what happened that night?" Nicholas asked.

She shook her head and squeezed his hand tighter. "I heard the fire bells and I could see the fire from the boardinghouse. I ran here as fast as I could, but I was too late. Only Nora Goode survived. Pretty Nora. They say she married you."

Nora? His mother's name was Nora.

Nicholas felt his heartbeat quicken. Was he finally going to learn the truth about his family after all these years?

"What did Nora look like?" Nicholas questioned. He held his breath—waiting for her answer.

"Shame on you. Not remembering what your own wife looked like. She had long brown hair and the prettiest green eyes. She had a sweet smile, I remember."

Yes, Nicholas thought. Brown hair and green eyes—like my mother. My mother was Nora Goode.

Nicholas's brain whirled with thoughts. So my father must have been Daniel Fear. That is why this poor woman thought I had returned from the dead. My father and I look so much alike she confused us.

It was my father I saw in my vision that night in

Shadow Cove, Nicholas realized. Not myself—my father!

At last! At last he knew his father's name. And his mother's true name. He knew his parents were Nora Goode and Daniel Fear.

"Thank you for talking to me," Nicholas said. He hesitated. "Don't you have any other place to live?" he asked quietly.

"This is the place for me. Near my Charles. Sometimes I see him. He visits me sometimes." The woman nodded emphatically. "Yes, he does. But not for long. He has to stay dead and so do you."

Nicholas pulled a few dollars out of his pocket and handed them to her. He needed the money—but she needed it more. "Maybe I can visit again."

The woman did not release his hand. "Please take me with you. I want to live with the dead. I want to live with my Charles."

"I am sorry, but I cannot," Nicholas told her. He gently pulled his hand free.

I know who I am, he thought as he walked back through the mansion. I know who I am.

My family lived here at one time. My father and mother spent time in this house. And my great-grandparents! Great-grandparents. Nicholas could hardly believe it.

Nicholas passed under the huge hole burned through the ceiling. He relished the feel of the rain pelting down on him. The rain washing away who he had once been. Washing away Nicholas Storm.

Lightning flashed. "I know who I am at last!" Nicholas cried over the booming thunder. "I am Daniel Fear's son."

He clenched his fists. "I am Nora Goode's son!"

He threw his head back.

"I am a Fear!" he shouted. "Nicholas Fear!"

Chapter 17

Nicholas Fear. He repeated the name to himself as he ran back down Fear Street, suitcase in hand.

Fear Street. A street named after *his* family. Even Rosalyn's father did not have a street named after him.

The rain pelted Nicholas, drenching him to the bone. But he did not care.

This is the place I will make my fortune, he thought. I know it. *Know* it.

The land I am running on belongs to me. My legacy from my father. I will build a house here. Bigger than any house in town.

Nicholas grinned when he reached the Fear Street sign. He rounded the corner and raced down the street lined with small houses. Lights glowed in the windows. He could see one family having their supper together.

He turned onto the main street. It stood almost deserted, the shops closed.

Nicholas caught sight of a man scurrying along the muddy sidewalk. He asked for directions to a boardinghouse before the man rushed past him.

Nicholas continued to imagine what his new life would be like as he headed to the boardinghouse. He would definitely buy an automobile, he decided, remembering the Runabout he had seen by the bank. He and Rosalyn would take a drive every Sunday.

And he would buy Rosalyn as many dresses as she wanted. She would be the most beautiful woman in town. Everyone would recognize them as they motored by. There go the Fears, they would whisper. The richest family in town.

Nicholas spotted the big blue house the man had described. He dashed up the steps, but hesitated to knock on the door.

I certainly do not look like the richest man in town today, Nicholas thought. He was soaked. His shirt had a tear in it, and his small suitcase appeared shabbier than ever. He wondered if the landlady would even give him a room.

The door squeaked as a teenage girl threw it open. A bright yellow ribbon held her blond hair behind her head. A few brown freckles dotted her nose. Her blue eyes twinkled as she smiled up at him.

"I am Betsy Winter. My mother owns the boardinghouse. I noticed you come up the walk. I hope you are looking for a room," she exclaimed.

Relieved, Nicholas returned her smile. "As a matter of fact, I am."

"Momma!" she called over her shoulder. "We have a new boarder!"

"Won't your mother want to ask me some questions?"

"I think you are handsome," Betsy replied. "That is all I need to know. Come on in."

Handsome! Nicholas felt his face grow warm. He hoped Betsy did not notice his embarrassment.

Nicholas stepped into a large parlor. Lace curtains hung at the windows. Carefully dusted porcelain figurines sat on tiny tables scattered throughout the room.

He felt awkward. Much too big and clumsy for the dainty room. And he was dripping all over the carpet.

A small woman bustled in. Nicholas noticed that her hair was the same blond as Betsy's, with a little gray streaked through it. Mrs. Winter also had a sprinkling of freckles across her nose.

"Momma, this is our new boarder. Isn't he sweet?" Betsy bounced up and down on her toes. Nicholas had never met a girl with so much energy and enthusiasm. She reminded him of a yellow puppy.

Mrs. Winter shoved a strand of hair back into her bun and laughed. "It seems Betsy has made my decision for me. Welcome to the boardinghouse, Mr.—?"

"Fear," Nicholas said. "I am Nicholas Fear." He relaxed. Both mother and daughter were so warm and friendly, he could not stay nervous.

Betsy squealed and dropped down on the sofa, her blue eyes wide. "Fear! Are you related to the crazy people who used to live in the mansion?"

"Betsy!" Mrs. Winter chided. "It is not polite to call people crazy." She smiled apologetically at Nicholas.

Nicholas suddenly realized he knew almost nothing about his family. He knew they once lived in a big house, on a street named after them. But he had no idea what kind of people they were.

"But the Fears *were* crazy, Momma," Betsy insisted. "Everybody thinks so."

"I have been told my great-grandparents used to live in that house," Nicholas answered slowly. "My father died there."

"Now that I think about it, you do look remarkably like Daniel Fear," Mrs. Winter said. "We need to get you settled in your room right away. You are soaked."

Nicholas felt grateful to Mrs. Winter for changing the subject.

"I will take him." Betsy jumped up from the sofa and grabbed his suitcase.

"Come down to the kitchen once you dry off and I will give you something to eat," Mrs. Winter called as he started after Betsy. "And mind you do not let my daughter talk your ear off," she added.

"I know you will like it here," Betsy said. "We started renting rooms about three years ago. After my father died. He never had a lot of money, so we were not left with much."

Nicholas had never heard someone talk so much or so fast.

"Not like your family," Betsy rushed on as she reached the top of the stairs and led him down a long hallway. "I imagine they left tons of money. They owned all that land. And that huge mansion."

Betsy stopped and opened the door to a small bedroom. "This is yours. You share a bath two doors down. I will leave you some towels. I am so happy you are staying here."

Betsy hurried away with a little wave. Then she spun back to face him. "I hope I did not offend you by talking about your family. Momma always says I do not think before I speak. Please tell me you are not angry."

Nicholas shook his head and smiled at her. How could anyone be angry with Betsy? It was clear she just blurted out whatever popped into her mind. "I hope you will tell me more about my family later," he answered. "Do you know about the fire?"

"It happened before I was born," Betsy told him. "But everyone knows about it. *Poof!* In one big fire, all the Fears were gone. And everything went with them. Except the land. Andrew Manning owns it now. He is the wealthiest man in Shadyside. I heard—"

"Betsy!" her mother called. "Come down here and leave Mr. Fear in peace, please."

Betsy winked at Nicholas. "Yes, Momma," she answered.

As he watched Betsy scamper down the stairs, Nicholas decided that first thing in the morning he would make a call on Mr. Andrew Manning. Mr. Manning might be the wealthiest person in town now . . . but not for long, Nicholas promised himself. Not for long.

Betsy was right, Nicholas thought as he peered up at the Mannings' house the next morning. Mr. Manning must be rich.

Nicholas pushed open the huge wrought-iron gate and walked up the pebbled path. He wondered how much of Mr. Manning's wealth came from the Fear land. How much of it rightfully belonged to Nicholas.

He climbed the steps of the wooden porch, then grabbed the brass door knocker and gave it three sharp raps.

"I am coming!" a shrill voice cried. "I am coming!"

The door swung open. A wrinkled-faced woman with snow-white hair stared at Nicholas. Her gray eyes widened. Then she uttered a loud shriek of terror.

"What has happened now?" a short man bellowed as he strode up behind the woman. He led her to a kitchen chair, gesturing for Nicholas to follow.

"I apologize. Somehow I frightened—" Nicholas began.

"Take deep breaths," he ordered the woman, ignoring Nicholas. She obediently sucked in a deep breath and let it out slowly.

"Mrs. Baker is always having these little fits," the man explained to Nicholas. "Yesterday, she fainted because the butcher sent the chickens over without cutting off their heads. Said their little eyes were staring at her."

"Mr. Manning," the woman gasped. "It is Daniel Fear, risen from the grave!"

"Nonsense," Andrew Manning insisted.

"It is him I tell you! I would recognize him anywhere!" Mrs. Baker cried, her voice growing higher and higher.

"Then he is certainly well-preserved, isn't he, Mrs. Baker? I wish the years had been as kind to me." He turned his attention back to Nicholas. "Who are you, young man?"

"Nicholas Fear," he answered, fighting to sound calm and confident. "I am Daniel Fear's son."

"You see, Mrs. Baker. There is a logical explanation for everything," Mr. Manning scolded.

"I seem to be scaring people all over town," Nicholas admitted. "I never knew my father and I had such a similar appearance."

Nicholas took a deep breath. "I wanted to speak with you about the property in the area, Mr. Manning," he added.

"Wonderful. I enjoy company in the morning. Mrs. Baker, fetch us some coffee and some of your strawberry tarts when you have recovered yourself."

Mr. Manning led the way down the hall. Nicholas peered into each room they passed. Thick draperies covered the windows. Oil paintings hung on the walls. Dark mahogany furniture filled each room.

Power, Nicholas thought in awe. *This is what wealth and power look like. This is what I want.*

He followed Mr. Manning into the study. Mr. Manning sat down in a large leather chair behind his desk. He gestured to a smaller chair in front of him. Nicholas sat down.

Before either of them could speak, Mrs. Baker bustled in with the coffee and strawberry tarts. She set them on the corner of the desk, careful to stay away from Nicholas.

"Silly woman," Mr. Manning muttered. He smiled at Nicholas. "She has been with me since my wife died, and practically raised my daughter, Ruth. So I suppose I must put up with her."

Nicholas heard the affection in Mr. Manning's voice. *Maybe this will be easier than I thought. Maybe he will understand.*

Andrew reached for a tart and shoved it into his mouth. "Delicious. Try one, dear boy," he mumbled.

"No, thank you," Nicholas replied. Nicholas felt his stomach knot. He shifted in the chair, the leather creaking.

Mr. Manning licked the strawberry jam off his fingers. "You wanted to discuss property. Tell me what I can do for you."

Nicholas took a deep breath. He leaned forward,

his elbows digging into his thighs. "You can return to me what is rightfully mine."

Andrew lifted his thick, gray eyebrows. "And what would that be?"

"My inheritance—the fortune that belongs to the Fear family."

Andrew Manning threw his head back and burst out laughing.

Chapter 18

Nicholas clenched his fists as Mr. Manning let out another roar of laughter. He felt as though he were suffocating. Rage burned through him.

"My dear boy," Mr. Manning said as he gasped for breath. "There is no fortune."

"You are lying!" Nicholas shot back. "You do not want to give up the money that belongs to me!"

"That is a serious accusation," Mr. Manning answered calmly. "You are welcome to talk to the president of the bank—and anyone else. They will all tell you the same thing. You have no inheritance—except for huge back taxes on the land."

Nicholas stood, his knees weak with shock. He could not stay in the room another minute. He could not allow Mr. Manning to see how shaken he was.

"Sit back down," Mr. Manning ordered. "Please. I should not have laughed."

Nicholas slowly returned to his chair. "Back taxes?" he whispered, the anger giving way to despair.

Mr. Manning nodded. "I am afraid so. I had grand plans to build houses along each side of the street. Beautiful houses."

The older man shook his head. "But I underestimated how superstitious people can be. No one wanted to live on Fear land. They had all heard one wild story or another. I had to abandon the project."

Mr. Manning's chair scraped against the floor as he got up. He placed his hand on Nicholas's shoulder. "I truly am sorry."

"I know," Nicholas rasped. "I just . . ." He sighed deeply.

"Had hopes," Mr. Manning finished for him. "And dreams."

"Something like that," Nicholas agreed as he turned to face Mr. Manning. "I am sorry to have bothered you."

"No bother," Mr. Manning said. He opened the French doors leading to the garden. "Step outside for some fresh air. You look as though you need some."

He and Nicholas walked onto the patio. Mr. Manning breathed deeply. "I love the way the air smells in the morning."

Nicholas stared out at the trees and flower beds until he felt in control of himself. Then he stuck out his hand to Mr. Manning. "Thank you again. I am sure you are very busy, so—"

Mr. Manning gave Nicholas's hand a firm shake.

"What are your plans now?" he asked. "Will you return home?"

Nicholas shook his head. He could not go back to Shadow Cove a poor man. "No," he replied. "There is a girl back home I want to marry. But her father will not give his consent. He wants his daughter to marry a wealthy man."

Nicholas hesitated a moment. He felt ashamed to tell Mr. Manning the rest. "I promised Rosalyn—that is her name—that I would return with a fortune big enough to convince her father to change his mind," he admitted. "I thought it would be so easy."

"Every father tends to think no man is good enough for his daughter," Mr. Manning told him sympathetically. "I know I worry about finding someone good enough for my Ruth. Someone who will love her and make her happy."

Nicholas shook his head. "Rosalyn's father is different. He does not care how much I love Rosalyn. He only cares about how much money I have. I have to prove to him that I can earn as much as any other man."

Mr. Manning studied Nicholas for a moment. "I have a sawmill. You can work there. Learn the trade," he offered. "The pay is fair. A man with ambition could make something of himself in my sawmill."

Nicholas felt a little hope return. A job in a mill was not what he had in mind when he left Shadow Cove. But it was a start. "I am a man with ambition," he declared.

"Then I expect to see you at seven o'clock sharp

tomorrow morning," Mr. Manning said. "Anyone can give you directions to the sawmill."

"Thank you. You will not be disappointed," Nicholas promised. Mr. Manning showed him through the house and he hurried down the walkway toward the wrought-iron gate.

He clanged the gate shut behind him and took a few steps down the street. Then he stopped and turned back. He waved to Mr. Manning. "See you at seven!" he called. "Even earlier!"

Mr. Manning waved back. "Seven is fine," he yelled before he returned to his study.

I will work hard, Nicholas promised himself, staring up at the Mannings' elegant home. I will learn everything about the lumber business. And someday I will have a house as large as this one. Someday I will regain the Fear property.

A piercing scream rang out behind him.

Before Nicholas could turn around, something rammed into him. Threw him to the ground.

The air rushed out of his lungs with a *whoosh.*

Burning pain shot through his side.

Something heavy pressed down on his chest.

Dots of light burst in front of his eyes.

He could not breathe. Could not breathe.

Chapter 19

Pain burst through Nicholas's chest as he gasped for air.

Someone moaned.

He forced his eyes open.

A bicycle lay beside him. A tall, skinny girl was sprawled over his chest.

No wonder I cannot breathe, he thought.

She lifted her head and flung her tangled hair out of her eyes. She had black eyes. Black eyes as lifeless as the eyes of the fish Nicholas used to catch.

The girl pushed herself off his chest and scrambled to her feet. "I am sorry. It is all my fault. I am so clumsy. Are you hurt?" she asked.

Nicholas sat up. "No, I am fine. But what about you? Are you hurt?"

"No. Do not worry about me. I am so sorry. I didn't know you were going to stop in the middle of the road," she explained. "And I am too slow. I could not stop in time." She reached down and helped Nicholas to his feet.

Her hand felt moist and cold. Like holding hands with a fish, Nicholas thought.

He could not help comparing this girl with Rosalyn. Rosalyn's eyes were deep brown. They reflected every emotion. And her skin was warm and smelled like roses.

"I should have watched where I was going," Nicholas said, trying to be polite. The girl could not help her strange black eyes and clammy skin.

He released the girl's hand and brushed the dirt off his clothes.

She reached down and pulled her bicycle back onto its wheels. "I have never seen you before," she said quickly, her eyes lowered. "Are you new in town?"

"Yes, I arrived yesterday. I am Nicholas Fear."

"I hope our next meeting is not so painful," the girl added, her eyes still on the ground. "I must practice using the brakes."

She is shy, Nicholas realized. "And I must practice looking where I am going, Miss—"

"Oh! Manning," she answered. She sounded startled. "Ruth Manning."

"I just met your father," Nicholas said. "He gave me a job."

"That is wonderful," Ruth exclaimed. "I feel much better now. At least one person in my family gave you a suitable welcome to Shadyside."

"You must stop worrying about me. I am perfectly

fine," Nicholas insisted. "Good-bye, Miss Manning. I hope to see you again."

"Oh, Mr. Fear?" Ruth hesitated.

"What is it?" Nicholas asked.

"You might want to button your shirt before you go," she said.

Nicholas stared down. Three of the buttons had come undone when he fell. He laughed. "Thank you. I would not make a good first impression walking around town like this."

He began to rebutton his shirt. "What is that you wear?" Ruth asked, pointing to the amulet.

"It was a gift," he answered. "A gift from my fiancée."

"I have never seen anything so beautiful," she whispered. She reached out with trembling fingers and flipped the amulet over. "Dominatio per malum," she read. "Power through evil."

For the first time, her gaze met his. He shivered as he stared into her expressionless black eyes.

"Do you believe in evil, Mr. Fear?" Ruth asked solemnly.

"I believe in power," he answered as he removed the disk from her grasp and buttoned his shirt.

Nicholas arrived for work at sunrise the next morning. He watched as several men turned cranks to lift the large doors.

While he waited, Nicholas studied everything he could see. He wanted to learn faster than anyone Mr. Manning had ever hired.

The sawmill had been built beside a wide, flowing river. The water rushed by and turned a paddle wheel. The wheel ran the machinery in the mill.

The other workers trooped inside as soon as the doors were open, and Nicholas followed them. Huge machines and large circular saws filled the building. He touched his finger to the jagged edge of one saw blade.

"Careful," someone called. "You have to treat the saws as if they are always running. You could lose a finger if you do not."

Nicholas turned around. A short, lean guy about Nicholas's age stood watching him with serious blue eyes.

"You are such an old woman, Jason," another worker joked. He looked like a human mountain. He stood over six feet tall, with a meaty, powerful build. He had bright red hair and green eyes.

"You must be the new worker Mr. Manning told us about," the redheaded man said. "I'm Ike. And my grandmother here is Jason. You will be working with us."

"I am Nicholas," he replied.

"I am not an old woman," Jason told Nicholas, shooting a hard look at his big friend. "It is smart to treat the saws as if they are dangerous—even when they are off. I just thought you should know that. Last month—"

"So, Nicholas, you ever work in a sawmill before?" Ike interrupted.

"No," Nicholas admitted.

"Nothing to it." He winked. "Just make sure you count your fingers at the end of the day. Jason counts his every night. He worries about his fingers so much that he failed to notice the fact that he cut off three toes!"

Ike guffawed, and Nicholas could tell Jason was trying not to smile. It is clear these two have been friends for a long time, he thought.

"I did not cut off my toes," Jason protested halfheartedly.

"Take off your shoes and prove it!" Ike challenged. "No, wait. Here comes the boss's daughter. You do not want to offend her with the aroma of your feet."

"And you do not want to offend me with your flapping lips. You may be as big as a bear, but I can knock you down to size and you know it."

Jason grinned at Nicholas. "Do not be fooled by the size of him. I have to wrestle him to the ground every few days to keep him in his place. You can do it, too. It is easy."

Ike growled. Then smiled sweetly as Ruth walked by.

"Good morning," Ruth murmured as she stopped beside them.

"Have you met Nicholas?" Ike asked. "It is his first day."

"Yes, we have met." Ruth gave Nicholas a small smile, without quite looking at him.

"Ike, would you find someone to sweep the floor, please?" Ruth asked. "The sawdust is too high."

"Sure, Miss Manning," Ike answered, tipping his cap.

"Does she work here?" Nicholas asked, when Ruth continued on her way.

"She takes care of the books," Ike answered as he reached for a broom. "She is as plain as a plank of wood and never has much to say. I think she is a perfect match for Jason," he teased.

Jason snorted, shoving his blond hair off his face. "I am not the one who falls all over her," he shot back. "Sure, Miss Manning. Whatever you say, Miss Manning," he mimicked.

Ike laughed good-naturedly and handed the broom to Nicholas. "The new guy sweeps."

Nicholas began making piles of sawdust. Then he heard someone call his name. He glanced up and saw Betsy hurrying toward him, her blond hair bouncing around her shoulders.

Several of the other workers stopped what they were doing to watch her pass by, but Betsy never took her eyes off Nicholas. She thrust a brown box with red hearts drawn on it into his hands. "Your lunch!" she explained. "I made it just for you and you forgot it this morning."

"Oh, isn't that sweet," Ike cooed, clasping his big, beefy hands in front of him.

"No lunch for me, Betsy?" Jason asked. "I thought you were going to help me grow as big and strong as Ike!"

"You made fun of what I brought last time, so you

are not getting anything else," Betsy answered. "Nicholas gets all my lunches from now on."

Betsy tossed her blond curls over her shoulder and smiled at Nicholas. "Mother says I should call you Mr. Fear, since you are a boarder. But I like Nicholas better! You do not mind, do you?"

Nicholas shook his head. Jason turned and stared at Nicholas, his blue eyes icy.

"Nicholas is handsomer than you and Ike put together, so I have decided to cook only for him!" Betsy teased Jason.

She did not appear to notice how serious Jason's expression had grown. But Nicholas did. He could see the muscles flexing in Jason's jaw.

"Betsy, you are looking for trouble flirting that way," Jason warned, his voice harsh. "You have to leave now. There is work to be done here."

Jason must really like Betsy, Nicholas thought. He is so jealous and all she did was bring me my lunch.

"All right," Betsy agreed with a sigh. "See you tonight," she called to Nicholas. Then she scampered out of the mill, getting a few more appreciative glances from the men.

Nicholas felt the back of his neck prickle. He had the sensation of someone watching him. Staring at him. He glanced up, and found Ruth standing at the window of one of the second-floor offices. He waved to her, but she turned away.

Poor Ruth, he thought. She must feel bad seeing all

the men goggling over Betsy. I bet no man has ever looked at her that way.

Nicholas shrugged and returned to sweeping up the sawdust.

By the end of his first day, Nicholas had decided he liked the lumber business.

Wood smells a lot better than fish, he thought as he strolled back to the boardinghouse. It had a fresh smell. He did not mind ending the day smelling like sawdust.

And the wood felt smooth—not slimy.

Nicholas heard a faint rustle in the bushes alongside the road. He stopped. The sound stopped, too.

He began to walk again. The rustling sound began again.

Is someone following me?

Nicholas knew almost no one in town. Who could be following him?

Pain jabbed the back of his head. Something fell to the ground with a thud.

A rock. Someone had thrown a rock at him!

Nicholas touched the back of his head and winced. Warm, sticky blood coated his fingers. He could feel more blood running down his neck.

He kicked the rock. It rolled twice, then stopped.

There is something tied around it, Nicholas realized.

Ignoring the pain in his head, he bent down and grabbed the rock. A piece of brown paper covered it. Nicholas pulled off the string and opened the paper.

"No," he whispered as he read the message. Who would do such a thing?

"Be afraid, Nicholas Fear," the note read. "You don't belong in Shadyside."

Chapter 20

Nicholas sucked in his breath. The gash in his scalp burned as Betsy dabbed alcohol on it.

"You have to be careful working at the sawmill. Accidents can happen so easily," she cautioned him.

"It did not happen at the sawmill," he said through clenched teeth. "It happened while I was walking home."

Betsy put the alcohol on the kitchen table and sat in the chair next to his. "Someone attacked you?"

He shrugged. "Someone threw a rock at me. With this note wrapped around it." He dug the crumpled note out of his pocket and handed it to her.

Her blue eyes widened as she read the words.

"I do not know why anyone would threaten me like that. I can think of nothing I have done to cause such hatred." Nicholas's brow furrowed.

"Actually, Nicholas, it could have been anyone," Betsy admitted. "People in Shadyside have always hated the Fears. The Goodes especially."

"Why?" Nicholas asked. "Why would anyone hate an entire family?"

Betsy sighed. "There is an old feud between the Goodes and the Fears. I do not know how it began. But there is much hatred on both sides." Betsy hesitated, her blue eyes filled with concern for Nicholas.

"Tell me," Nicholas urged.

"It is said that the Fears practiced dark magic. Many people—not just the Goodes—claim they performed strange ceremonies in their mansion. Ceremonies that required blood. That is why the mansion is set so far back from the street—the Fears did not want anyone to see what they did there."

Nicholas did not know what to say. He stared down at his hands. He did not want Betsy to notice how badly her story had upset him.

"I should wash off this blood," he muttered. He had kept one hand over his head wound all the way back to the boardinghouse. His hands were caked with dried blood.

Nicholas stood and crossed to the sink. He ran water over his hands. The dry, brown blood grew thick, sticky, and bright red. The blood's rusty scent filled his nostrils.

Their ceremonies involved blood, he thought. What were they doing inside the mansion?

He lathered soap over his hands and scrubbed his skin viciously. Scrubbed it until it was raw.

Then he turned the water off. But he did not take his seat beside Betsy.

What else would he discover about the Fear family? *His* family? "What else?" he asked in a low voice.

He heard Betsy's chair scrape against the floor as she stood up. She hurried over and placed her hand on his back.

He tensed.

"I heard that two of Simon and Angelica's children were found in the Fear Street Woods. All their bones had been removed. At least that is the story people tell."

Betsy hesitated again, then continued in a rush. "People say many of the Fears have died strange and horrible deaths. They say bad luck follows every member of the family. But I do not believe in bad luck," Betsy added firmly. "And neither should you."

Nicholas looked over his shoulder. "How do you know so much about my family?"

"I am a Goode—sort of. My mother was a Goode before she married my father."

Betsy reached around him and picked up a large knife. She ran her finger along the shiny edge.

Nicholas stiffened.

She stepped up to the counter and began chopping tomatoes. "Do not worry," she said. "I like Fears just fine."

She glanced over at him. "Of course, not everyone in my family does."

Nicholas watched the saw's teeth bite into the wood. The saw had an endless appetite.

That is why you must pay attention, Nicholas ordered himself. All morning his eyes had wandered away from his work and over to the other men. He studied their faces, trying to decide if one of them had thrown the rock.

Ike fed another board to Nicholas. Nicholas and Ike were working by themselves today. Jason had teamed up with a man whose usual partner was sick.

Nicholas felt the board quiver as it met the saw. When the end of the board slid through the blade, Ike whistled.

Nicholas glanced up. Ike rubbed his stomach. Nicholas smiled. Ike was hungry. Nicholas nodded and turned off the saw.

"I will meet you outside!" Ike yelled as he picked up his lunch.

Nicholas grabbed his small cardboard box and headed after Ike. Today Betsy had drawn arrows through the red hearts. He hoped Jason did not notice.

Nicholas paused by the pile of wood he and Ike would cut that afternoon and checked each piece carefully. Ike had explained what could happen if a saw jammed on a knothole. And Nicholas did not want to take any chances.

He ran his fingers over one of the boards. The wood was good quality, smooth and fine. This is the type of wood that should be used to build houses on Fear Street, Nicholas thought.

He continued outside and found Ike sitting on a log. Nicholas dropped down beside him. "Is Jason eating with us?"

Ike shrugged. "He said he had something to do."

"Do you think it bothers him that I live in the boardinghouse with Betsy and her mother?" Nicholas asked.

"That depends," Ike answered. "What did she pack her sweetheart today?" Ike asked.

"I am not her sweetheart," Nicholas grumbled.

"She thinks so," Ike said, his green eyes sparkling. He grabbed the box and peeked inside. "Mmmm-mmmm. Fried chicken. I would be happy to be her sweetheart if she cooked like this for me."

Nicholas gave Ike a piece of chicken, and they ate in silence—enjoying the food and the warm sun.

"Why don't we change places?" Ike suggested when they finished lunch. "I will work the saw and you feed me the boards."

"All right," Nicholas agreed as they returned to their station. "I checked the wood for knotholes before I left. I knew you were going to do it—but I wanted to check them, too."

"Turning into an old lady like Jason," Ike scolded. "I am kidding," he added. "It is smart to check things yourself."

Ike took his position beside the saw. "Watch for splinters as you feed me the boards," Ike advised. "They can hurt like crazy."

Ike flipped the switch. The saw whirred to life.

Nicholas picked up a plank and began guiding it toward Ike and the saw.

The whizzing saw bit into the wood.

Then it came to an abrupt halt.

Ike scowled. He put some pressure on the wood.

It did not budge.

Ike leaned closer.

The saw jumped free. It tore through the wood.

Ike uttered a long, deep moan of pain.

Blood sprayed into the air. It spattered across Nicholas's face. Soaked into his shirt.

Nicholas leapt over to the saw and shut it off.

"Get them for me! Get them for me!" Ike shrieked.

"What?" Nicholas yelled back. "I do not know what you want."

"My fingers!" Ike howled.

Chapter 21

Nicholas crouched down beside the saw. Blood gushed from Ike's hand, turning the sawdust on the floor bright red.

Nicholas heard Ike moaning. He groped through the wet sawdust. Searching, searching.

"My fingers!" Ike yelled again. Someone else shouted. The saws stopped one by one. Feet pounded up beside Nicholas.

Nicholas continued to search. The sawdust flew into his eyes, making it hard to see.

Then he saw them. All three fingers had flown to the other side of their worktable.

Nicholas stretched out under the table. His face pressed against the bloody sawdust. He could just reach them.

He jumped up, the fingers in his hand. They still felt

warm. "I have them, Ike! I have them all," Nicholas shouted.

Someone had wrapped a cloth around Ike's hand. But the blood had already soaked through it.

Nicholas tore off his shirt and pressed it against the stubs of Ike's fingers. Blood drenched the shirt in seconds.

Ike groaned low in his throat. Every freckle stood out against his pasty-white face.

"We will get you to a doctor," Nicholas promised.

Without warning, Jason shoved Nicholas aside. "I knew we could not trust you," he yelled. "This is your fault."

Glaring at Nicholas, Jason rewrapped Ike's bloody hand with his own shirt. "Go get the doctor," he snapped at one of the other men.

Jason led Ike to a corner of the room and had him stretch out on the floor. He held Ike's hand straight up.

Nicholas felt guilt wash over him.

Was it my fault? he wondered. Did I do something wrong? I checked the boards before we went to lunch. I checked the boards. They didn't have any knotholes.

Nicholas noticed some of the other men giving him angry looks. They should not blame me. The same thing would have happened to me if Ike had been feeding me the boards, he thought.

A chill raced through Nicholas. He remembered the rock someone had thrown at him the day before. The rock with the note warning Nicholas he did not belong in Shadyside.

Did someone plant the board to cause the accident? Ike and I did not decide to switch places until after lunch. Did someone hope *I* would be hurt?

The next day, the sawmill felt too quiet. Even with the noise of the machinery.

The doctor did not know when Ike would be able to return to work. Or if he would be able to return at all.

Nicholas felt horrible. Ike was his first real friend in Shadyside. He made the job fun. And he was willing to teach Nicholas everything.

Nicholas would do anything to make it up to Ike. But there was nothing to do.

Nicholas had been assigned to work with Jason. Jason only spoke to him to give him orders. The other men did not speak to him at all.

Nicholas could hardly believe Ike would not come up behind him, teasing him about Betsy's lunches. He did not know what he would do if Ike could never come back to work.

He knew most of the men blamed him. He blamed himself a lot of the time. He had checked the boards so carefully. But maybe he had missed the knothole.

He felt sick inside every time he pictured Ike's hand. Or the way Ike's face looked when he screamed for his fingers.

Nicholas searched the grain of each board Jason fed him. He wanted to be sure no one arranged an "accident" for him.

Around noon, Jason stopped feeding the boards and walked away without a word.

I suppose that means it is time for lunch, Nicholas thought. Very nice, Jason. He turned off the saw. The buzzing continued to ring in his ears.

Nicholas wandered outside and sat on the log he had shared with Ike the day before. He felt lonely.

I need Rosalyn here, he thought. I need someone to talk to.

He heard footsteps and glanced up. Mr. Manning walked toward him. Ruth scurried along behind her father.

Is he going to fire me? Nicholas wondered. Does he blame me for Ike's accident, too?

Mr. Manning dropped onto the log. He exhaled a deep breath. "Have you met my daughter?" he asked.

"Yes, Father," Ruth replied before Nicholas could answer. "I ran into him before he began working at the mill."

Ruth glanced at him shyly, and they smiled at their secret joke.

"Ruth does all my paperwork," Mr. Manning said. He clapped his hand on Nicholas's shoulder. "She is a sharp girl. She has a head for numbers."

Isn't he going to ask me anything about the accident? Nicholas wondered.

"Do you know much about sawmills?"

"I am learning a little more each day," Nicholas answered, still feeling puzzled.

Mr. Manning beamed. "Good. My grandfather built this sawmill. He passed it on to my father who passed it on to me. I will pass it on to Ruth when the time comes. She will pass it on to her children. Do you like Shadyside?"

Nicholas blinked at the abrupt change of subject. "Yes, sir."

"It is a good place for a man to settle down. If he can find the right woman." He winked and tilted his head toward Ruth.

He wants me to take an interest in his daughter, Nicholas realized. That is why he came over.

"Mmmhmm," Nicholas murmured. He did not want to offend his employer. But he did not want to encourage Mr. Manning either.

Nicholas gazed over at Ruth. She stared at the ground, her head bowed. He thought he could see a faint blush on her cheeks.

She is embarrassed, he thought. He felt sorry for her. What girl would want to hear her father trying to bribe a man into courting her?

Ruth raised her dull black eyes, as if she felt him staring at her. "Sorry," she mouthed, shaking her head slightly.

Nicholas rolled his eyes, trying to show her he understood how parents could be.

"Ruth is my pride—"

"Father, have a sandwich," Ruth interrupted. She pulled one out of a box and handed it to him.

Nicholas bit back a laugh. That is one way to keep him quiet, he thought. Keep his mouth full.

Ruth pulled out another sandwich for herself and offered one to Nicholas.

"No, thank you," he said. "I have my own lunch."

He pulled out his lunch box. Betsy had drawn some roses between the hearts. He felt silly letting Ruth and Mr. Manning see it.

Mr. Manning was too busy eating to comment. He consumed his sandwich in four bites. Ruth handed him another before he could ask for one.

Mr. Manning nudged Nicholas with his elbow. "You see, she knows how to look after a man."

"Father—" Ruth began to protest weakly. She stopped and stared at her father's face. "Are you all right?" she asked. She sounded frightened.

Nicholas turned toward Mr. Manning. His face had a greenish cast to it. And little beads of sweat stood out on his forehead. "You do look ill," Nicholas said.

"Nonsense," Mr. Manning grumbled. He pulled out a silk handkerchief and wiped away the sweat. "I merely ate too fast. Nothing to worry about."

"Are you enjoying your lunch, Nicholas?" a high voice called out. Betsy. She rushed over, her blond hair bouncing on her shoulders.

Nicholas smiled at her. She wore a white dress with red polka dots. Ribbons and lace covered every available spot. Rosalyn would never wear a dress like that, he thought. She told him she thought they made girls look like big dolls.

And Ruth would look ridiculous in such a dress. The bright polka dots would only emphasize her shyness and her dead, black eyes.

But on Betsy the dress was perfect. "The lunch is delicious," he told her. "Thank you for making it for me."

"I like doing things for you," Betsy told him.

Nicholas heard Mr. Manning give an annoyed snort.

"You look very pretty today," Ruth said softly.

"Thank you," Betsy answered. "It is sweet of you to say so."

Betsy straightened the row of lace around one wrist and looked at Nicholas expectantly.

"Ruth is right," Nicholas said. He did not want to hurt Betsy's feelings. "It is a nice dress."

I hope Betsy does not think I am flirting with her. I will make sure and tell her all about Rosalyn tonight, Nicholas promised himself. Perhaps they will even become friends when I bring Rosalyn to Shadyside.

"I am going to bake my special sticky buns just for you to have with your supper this evening," Betsy told him in her usual mile-a-minute fashion. "And I—"

"Betsy!" Jason yelled. He leaned against a tree near the entrance to the mill. "Come here!"

She pouted. "Guess I better go see what he wants." She winked at Nicholas. "Hurry home after work. My mother has gone to visit her sister, so the two of us can have dinner alone—after I serve the other boarders."

She ambled over to Jason. Jason glared over the top of Betsy's head at Nicholas. Then he took Betsy by the shoulders and talked to her with a grim expression on his face.

Warning her to stay away from me, I am sure, Nicholas thought.

* * *

Nicholas rushed out of the sawmill as soon as he guided the last board through the saw.

He could not wait to get away from the men's hostile glares. No one had openly accused him, but he knew most of the other workers held him responsible for Ike's accident.

Besides, Nicholas thought, Betsy wanted me to be home early.

He hurried to the boardinghouse and circled around to the kitchen door. The scent of yeast greeted him before he even opened it.

Nicholas grinned. It smelled as if Betsy had been very busy.

He shoved open the kitchen door and stepped inside. Waves of heat hit him in the face.

How could she stand to have the kitchen so hot? She must have had the stove on for hours.

"Betsy?" Nicholas called.

The smell of the yeast was almost overpowering in the kitchen. But Nicholas noticed another smell underneath the yeast.

The sweet smell of cinnamon and sugar mixed with something . . . rotten.

"Betsy?" Nicholas yelled.

Then he saw her.

"Nooooo!" he screamed.

Betsy was crumpled on the kitchen floor. Her hands tied behind her back.

Chapter 22

Nicholas dashed over to Betsy. He untied her hands, tugging impatiently at the rope.

Then he gently rolled her over onto her back.

Nicholas's stomach twisted inside him as he stared down at her.

Betsy's face. Her pretty little freckled face. It was swollen. Horribly swollen.

Nicholas could hardly see her eyes. The skin around them had swollen so much they were almost completely covered.

"Can you hear me, Betsy?" Nicholas called. He picked up her wrist, trying to find a pulse.

Then he noticed something thick and white pushing its way out of her mouth. Nicholas dropped her wrist. He parted her lips and teeth.

The gooey white substance billowed out of her mouth.

Dough.

Nicholas checked her nose. Thick white dough filled it, too.

Someone had stuffed Betsy's nose and mouth with dough. And left her by the stove with her hands tied behind her back.

As the dough rose, she suffocated.

"Oh, Betsy, I am so sorry," he whispered hoarsely. He stood, not certain what he should do.

Who could have done this to Betsy? What kind of enemies could a girl like Betsy have?

Suddenly Nicholas remembered Jason grabbing Betsy by the shoulders. Jason appeared so angry today. Could he be jealous enough to . . .

No, Nicholas told himself. He had only known Jason for a few days, but he knew Jason could not have done this horrible thing. Not careful Jason. Jason who always followed the rules.

The sickly sweet odor hit his nose again. And this time he recognized it. The smell of decay. The smell of death.

Nicholas staggered out of the kitchen, slamming the door behind him.

He flopped down on the grass alongside the house and sucked in deep gulps of air. Trying to force the smell of death out of his nose and lungs.

The smell made him think of his mother. Of the night she died. The night she begged him never to leave Shadow Cove.

His mother had been so careful to keep him away

from Shadyside. She never even told him his true name. Did she believe in the bad luck of the Fears? Nicholas wondered.

A horrible thought flashed through Nicholas's mind. Would Betsy still be alive if she had not invited a Fear into her home?

Would Ike's accident have occurred if Nicholas had stayed in Shadow Cove?

What would happen next? Who would be hurt next time? Did a horrible death await Nicholas himself in Shadyside?

Now Nicholas understood why someone had thrown a rock at him. He had only been in town a few days, but he seemed to have brought the Fear bad luck back to Shadyside.

Nicholas plowed his hands through his hair, his fingernails scraping his scalp. He did not know what to do, where to go. Who would want to help him?

Mr. Manning. Maybe Mr. Manning could help him figure things out. At least he did not blame Nicholas for Ike's accident. And he had given Nicholas a job without knowing anything about him.

Nicholas climbed to his feet and headed for the road. Then he stopped. There was something he needed to do before he could leave.

Nicholas forced himself to go back into the kitchen. He jerked the tablecloth off the table and gently spread it over Betsy.

Then he walked out the door without looking back.

* * *

Nicholas ran all the way to the Mannings' house. He ran hard, arms and legs pumping. His lungs burned.

But he could not run fast enough to escape the vision of Betsy's bloated face. Or the feeling that somehow he was responsible.

Nicholas slammed through the Mannings' black wrought-iron gate and hurried up to the front door.

He grabbed the door knocker and rapped it several times. Mrs. Baker slowly opened the door halfway and stared up at him, a frightened expression on her face.

"It is Nicholas Fear, Mrs. Baker. May I see Mr. Manning?"

"He's not well this evening," she answered, sounding doubtful.

"Please. It is very important that I speak with him," Nicholas begged.

She opened the door a little farther. "Come in, then."

The gaslights flickered as he entered the foyer. "Follow me," Mrs. Baker instructed.

Mrs. Baker led Nicholas up a shadowy staircase. She stopped beside a polished oak door. "In there."

Nicholas tapped on the door, then stepped inside.

Mr. Manning was in bed, the comforters pulled up to his chin. "My dear boy, it is so good to see you," he called.

Nicholas crossed the room. Mr. Manning held out his hand, and Nicholas shook it. He could feel the older man's hand shaking. And it felt cold. Too cold.

Nicholas sat down in the chair beside the bed. Mr.

Manning's appearance frightened him. The man's skin had turned a sickly green, worse than it had been at lunch. Sweat beaded his brow. He licked his chapped lips.

"I am sorry that you are feeling ill," Nicholas said.

Mr. Manning rolled his head from side to side. "Just a cold or some such. I will be up and about as good as new in a day or so. What brings you here this evening?"

Nicholas did not know what to say. "Betsy is dead," he finally blurted out. Then he described everything he had seen at the boardinghouse.

"I did not know what to do," Nicholas concluded. "I did not know where to go."

"You did right in coming here," Mr. Manning assured him.

He rolled to his side and grabbed Nicholas's hand. He squeezed it hard, with more strength than Nicholas thought the older man possessed.

"You must stay here tonight," Mr. Manning said urgently. "Please. We have a spare room. What if someone comes after my dear Ruth? I am too ill to protect her. Please stay until I have regained my health."

Nicholas nodded. "You have been so kind to me. How can I refuse?"

He pushed himself to his feet. "I will let you rest now," Nicholas said. He did not like the raspy sound of Mr. Manning's breathing.

"Send Mrs. Baker to notify the preacher of Betsy's death," Mr. Manning wheezed. "I need you here.

Ruth is not safe. Not after what happened to poor Betsy."

Nicholas and Ruth attended Betsy's funeral together. It was the only way he could keep his promise to Mr. Manning—and do what he thought Betsy would want him to.

The service seemed to last forever. But at least the coffin was closed. Nicholas wanted to remember Betsy's face before her murder, not swollen and bruised.

Nicholas felt tears prick his eyes. He heard Ruth crying softly beside him, and Mrs. Winter sobbing in the first pew.

He turned his head slightly. Jason sat across the aisle from him, his blue eyes locked on Nicholas. His mouth was set in a grim line, his jaws clenched together.

When the service ended, Nicholas stood and hurried Ruth out of the church.

He needed to be out in the sun. Out in the light.

Nicholas felt a strong hand grab him and spin him around.

He stared into Jason's unforgiving face.

"We should have been burying you today—not my cousin," Jason growled.

Chapter 23

Nicholas's heart pounded in his ears. So loud it was the only thing he could hear.

Jason is Betsy's cousin—does that mean he is a Goode? Is that why he hates me so much?

Jason moved closer, his face inches away from Nicholas's. "You killed Betsy," he snarled.

Nicholas did not back away. He stared right into Jason's eyes. "I did not kill your cousin," he declared, slowly and deliberately.

"Nothing but evil can come of a Goode mixing with a Fear," Jason insisted. "I am a Goode. I know my family history. I know what the Fears have done to the Goodes. I warned Betsy that bad luck follows all the Fears, but she would not listen."

Nicholas glanced down and noticed that Jason's hands had curled into fists. "Hit me, if that will make you feel better," Nicholas challenged.

He heard Ruth gasp behind him.

He moved even closer to Jason. "It will not bring Betsy back, but go ahead."

Every muscle in Jason's body seemed to tighten. Nicholas could see a vein in Jason's head pulsing.

"Watch your back, Nicholas Fear," Jason said softly. "Because I promise you I will watch it. I will watch it as you leave this town."

He turned and walked away.

Nicholas glanced around. People were staring at him. Some looked angry. Some looked frightened. Some looked curious.

How many of you are Goodes? he wanted to ask. How many of you hate me simply because my last name is Fear?

He stared back at the crowd, meeting each pair of eyes directly. Maybe bad luck *did* follow the Fears. But Nicholas did not kill Betsy.

He did not stuff her mouth full of dough and leave her to suffocate. No, someone else in Shadyside did that. Someone evil.

One by one, people turned and walked away.

"Let's go," Nicholas muttered to Ruth.

Nicholas did not feel like talking. He was glad Ruth kept her opinions to herself as they made their way home.

When they reached the big iron gate in front of her house, Ruth put her hand on his arm. She looked up at him, her black eyes expressionless. "I am sorry," she said.

Ruth pushed open the gate and Nicholas followed her up the walkway.

"He does not know anything about me," Nicholas blurted out.

Ruth turned to face him. "Who?"

"Jason Goode. He does not know it, but my mother was a Goode. A Goode just like him," Nicholas declared.

"Why didn't you tell him?" she asked.

"Why should I explain anything to him!" Nicholas cried. "He accused me of killing Betsy without asking me one question. Everyone in this town has decided to hate me—and most of them have not even spoken to me yet."

"Not all," Ruth answered quietly.

Nicholas immediately felt bad. "No. You are right. You and your father have always been kind to me."

"My father thinks very highly of you," Ruth told him as they continued up to the house. "He wants to teach you all about the lumber business."

She is right, Nicholas thought. I will stay in Shadyside. I will work for Mr. Manning until I can pay off the back taxes on the Fear land. Then I will build a mansion so huge no one will ever forget there is a Fear in town.

Ruth opened the door and they walked inside. Nicholas helped Ruth off with her coat. He thought he noticed her blushing again.

Poor Ruth, Nicholas thought. She is not accustomed to the smallest attention from a man.

"I want to go check on Father," Ruth murmured, her eyes on the floor.

"Thank you for attending the funeral with me," Nicholas called as she crossed the room. Ruth gave a little nod in reply.

Nicholas hung Ruth's coat on the coatrack and removed his own.

A high wail of anguish sounded from upstairs.

Ruth!

Nicholas dropped his coat and dashed toward the stairs.

Ruth flew down them. Her face pale.

Tears streaming down her cheeks.

Nicholas grabbed her by the shoulders.

"What is it? What is it, Ruth?" he demanded.

"My father . . ."

Her lips quivered as she struggled to speak.

"My father is dead!"

Chapter 24

Nicholas sat next to Ruth on the parlor sofa a few hours later. She held a cup of tea in her hands, clutching it so tightly her knuckles were white.

Nicholas did not know what to say to her. So he just sat there in silence.

His mind raced over the events that had occurred since he arrived in Shadyside. So many deaths.

"I need to tell you something, Nicholas," Ruth said. She kept her eyes on her teacup.

"What is it?" Nicholas asked when she did not continue.

"I do not know how to say it," she admitted.

Nicholas felt like groaning. He wanted to be alone. He needed time to think. To figure out what he was going to do.

But he could not leave Ruth all by herself. "Tell me," he urged, trying to sound patient.

"It was my father's last wish that I marry you," Ruth said all in a rush.

"What?" He gasped.

"I was as shocked as you are." Ruth set her teacup down and turned to face him. "Last night I sat up with him. I was holding his hand. He started talking about dying."

Ruth sniffled. "I told him not to be silly. But he would not stop. He said that he wanted us to marry if anything happened to him."

Nicholas bowed his head and studied his shoes. I can hear the pain in her voice, he thought. I know she is hurting. I do not want to hurt her further.

But I cannot marry her.

Nicholas could not stand the thought of touching Ruth. Her cold, moist skin gave him chills. And her black fish eyes repulsed him.

I have to tell her about Rosalyn. Then she will understand. She will never have to know I would not have married her under any circumstances.

She twisted her hands in her lap. "I know you do not love me. I do not love you either."

Nicholas glanced at her, surprised. Perhaps she did not wish to marry him! He would convince her that her father would never want her to marry without love.

Nicholas felt his entire body relax.

"But we could be good company for each other," Ruth continued. "I have plenty of money. You would never have to worry about that." Ruth gazed at him pleadingly.

Nicholas stood and walked to the empty fireplace. Her voice held a deep sadness. He knew it would be lonely for her living in this large house all alone. But that was not his responsibility.

He turned to face Ruth. He decided not to mention Rosalyn. It might only make Ruth feel worse. "I am sorry," Nicholas said, "but I do not think either one of us would be happy if we married."

"You are probably right. But I had to ask," Ruth explained. She sighed. "I owed my father that much."

Relief flowed through Nicholas. "I will help you any way I can. I owe your father, too. He showed me much kindness."

Ruth rose to her feet and nodded. When she spoke her voice was calm and even. "You are welcome to stay in my home as my guest as long as you like."

"I'm not sure that would be proper," Nicholas began. "You are an unmarried—"

"No," Ruth interrupted. "My father would want you to stay here. If you will not do it for me, then please do it for him."

Reluctantly, Nicholas nodded. "Very well."

A pitiful smile touched her lips. "Thank you. I have a terrible headache. I think I shall go lie down for a while. Make yourself at home."

Nicholas watched as she slowly shuffled out of the room. *She looks so tired and frail,* he thought as he sat down. *Her father's death was a horrible blow to her.*

And to me, he added. *And to me.*

Mr. Manning could have thrown me out the day I

barged into his home demanding my fortune. Instead he gave me a job.

Nicholas's stomach cramped. Could Mr. Manning be another victim of the Fears' bad luck?

Disaster had come to every person who had been kind to Nicholas since he arrived in Shadyside. Ike. Betsy. Mr. Manning.

Wait, Nicholas thought. Slow down. Bad luck is not the only explanation.

No, there was an explanation that made much more sense.

Jason Goode.

Jason hates me. He hated me from the beginning.

No, Nicholas remembered. Not from the very beginning. From the moment he found out I was a Fear.

He was friendly until Betsy arrived with my lunch. I thought he was jealous that she was fussing over me—but he did not know I was a Fear until Betsy used my last name.

Discovering I was a Fear changed his attitude toward me. He hated me from that moment on because of the feud between our families.

Jason knew Mr. Manning liked me and was looking out for me. Jason could not stand that. So he killed Mr. Manning.

But what about Ike and Betsy? Jason cared for them both. Was his hatred of the Fears so great that he could maim his friend and kill his own cousin?

Jason probably planned for me to be running the saw, not Ike, Nicholas decided. I was running it that morning. And I was new. I bet Jason did not think Ike would allow me to switch jobs so soon.

Jason wanted to hurt *me*—not Ike.

But what about Betsy? Her death was no accident meant for him.

Jason tried to keep her away from me, Nicholas remembered. Every time he saw us together, he sent Betsy away,

Maybe Jason could not stand the thought of Betsy marrying a Fear. Maybe he thought she was better off dead than suffering the bad luck of the Fears.

Jason is not going to get away with it, Nicholas swore. If it is the last thing he does, Jason will admit the truth.

And he will pay for the lives he has taken.

Chapter 25

Nicholas did not knock on Jason's door. He slammed it open and walked inside.

Jason stood near the hearth, jabbing the fire with a poker. He spun around.

"What are you doing here?" Jason demanded. His lips twisted into a sneer.

"I came to get some answers," Nicholas shot back. "I want to know how you felt when you saw Ike's hand spurting blood—thanks to you."

Jason's eyes turned dark with anger and hatred. His body went rigid. "That was your fault!" Jason yelled. "You—"

"I want to know how it felt to kill Betsy," Nicholas interrupted. "Your own cousin."

"Nooooo!" Jason howled. "You killed Betsy." He lunged at Nicholas, the poker out in front of him.

Nicholas dove at Jason's knees. He knocked Jason to the floor.

Jason's head hit the hearthstone with a thud.

But the blow did not stop him. Jason rolled over and straddled Nicholas, pinning him to the floor.

Jason raised the poker high over his head. Aiming it at Nicholas's face.

He is going to kill me, Nicholas thought. He twisted his body with all his might. He knocked Jason off-balance.

The poker slid across the room and landed near the door.

Nicholas rolled free and jabbed his knee into Jason's stomach. He grabbed Jason by the throat.

"Confess!" Nicholas yelled.

Jason wheezed, trying to speak.

Nicholas relaxed his grip on Jason's neck. But kept his hands in position.

"Confess what?" Jason demanded.

"You killed Mr. Manning and Betsy! You set up the accident at the mill that maimed Ike. You wanted me out of Shadyside. So you attacked everyone who was kind to me."

"I wanted you out of Shadyside," Jason shot back. "And I threw the rock at your head—I wish now it had killed you. But that is all I did."

"You are a liar." Nicholas dug his knee deeper into Jason's stomach. Jason grunted in pain. "Tell me the truth!" Nicholas demanded.

"That is the truth. I would not kill innocent

people—even to hurt you. Especially Betsy." Jason's eyes filled with tears. "I loved Betsy. She never harmed anyone. Someone killed her. But it was not me."

Nicholas stared down at Jason. Could he be telling the truth?

"Who killed her, then?" Nicholas asked. He released Jason. They both climbed to their feet, watching each other warily.

"You did!" Jason insisted.

"No! You are blinded by your hatred. Why would I kill Mr. Manning or Betsy?"

"You killed Betsy because she was a Goode." Jason glared at Nicholas. "The Fears never needed a reason to kill the Goodes."

"My mother was a Goode," Nicholas protested. "A Goode who married a Fear."

"I do not believe you," Jason said. But the anger had gone out of his voice.

"I am going to find out who killed Betsy," Jason vowed. "If you lied to me, if I find out you killed her, then I will come after you."

"Fine," Nicholas agreed. "And if I find out that you are the murderer, I will kill you."

Nicholas and Jason stared at each other for a long moment. Then Nicholas turned to go.

Someone sprang out of the shadows beside the door and dashed toward Nicholas.

Chapter 26

Ruth! What was Ruth doing here?

Ruth ran past Nicholas.

With a screech, she grabbed the poker off the floor.

"Stop!" Nicholas yelled.

But Ruth did not hesitate. She reared back and plunged the poker into Jason's throat.

Blood spattered across the wall.

Jason fell backward onto the wooden floor.

He gasped for breath. A wet, sucking sound.

Nicholas rushed over and grabbed Ruth's shoulder. She twisted away from him with a snarl.

Nicholas watched in horror as Ruth turned the poker back and forth. Nicholas could hear it grinding into the floor below Jason's neck.

Ruth had stabbed Jason so hard the poker had popped through the back of his throat.

She was insane. Completely insane.

Ruth did not appear anything like the shy, awkward girl Nicholas had come to know. Had her father's death driven her to madness? Or had she kept it hidden away inside her always?

Bright red blood bubbled from Jason's mouth.

He stared blankly up at Nicholas. A surprised expression frozen on his face.

"Now you will have to marry me," Ruth said. She dropped the poker and turned around. A triumphant smile on her face.

"Ruth! Why did you kill him? *Why?*" Nicholas cried.

Ruth's eyes bored into his. No more staring shyly at the ground.

"I killed him so that if you do not marry me, you will hang for murder," she announced, her voice confident. "I will swear you killed Jason. And no one will take your word—the word of a stranger and a Fear—over mine."

"You killed Jason to force me to marry you?" Nicholas asked. He felt dizzy and sick.

She tilted her chin up defiantly. "I decided I wanted to marry you the day I ran into you on my bicycle. And I always get what I want."

"Even if it means killing an innocent man? What kind of woman are you?" Nicholas demanded.

His heartbeat pounded in his ears. He could hardly believe what he had seen with his own eyes. Ruth. Weak, mousy Ruth was a brutal killer.

"Jason is not the only one I killed to win you,"

Ruth said in a matter-of-fact tone. "I killed Betsy. I poisoned my father. And I arranged Ike's accident."

Jason's knees felt weak. What was she saying? How could she calmly explain that she had killed her own father?

"Why? Why, Ruth?"

"I did not want you to have anyone to turn to—except me. I wanted to make you absolutely powerless and friendless. So you would be forced to depend on me for everything," Ruth explained. She sounded pleased with herself.

She really sees nothing wrong with what she has done, Nicholas realized. She wanted something—and she did what she had to do to get it. Simple.

She is evil, Nicholas thought. Pure evil.

"You said it was your father's last wish that I marry you," Nicholas said weakly. He had actually pitied Ruth. Wondered how she would get along without her father.

She shrugged. "I am certain it would have been his last wish—if he had had the strength to wish for anything at all."

Ruth sauntered toward the door. "No more questions, Nicholas," she ordered. "None of the details matter now. What matters is that I want to get married right away."

"I will not marry you," Nicholas vowed. The thought of spending his life with Ruth sent a shudder through him.

"Oh, I think you will. The alternative is death," Ruth said flatly.

To Nicholas's amazement, tears welled up in Ruth's eyes and rolled down her cheeks. What was happening?

Ruth smiled up at him sweetly. "I can make myself cry whenever I want to, and I shall cry constantly on the witness stand. I will tell them how good my father was to you and how you repaid his kindness by poisoning him. I will tell the judge you killed Jason because he discovered the truth."

She wiped the tears away and her eyes were dry instantly.

She would do it, too, Nicholas thought. If I do not do exactly as she wishes, she will have me hanged. How could he get away from her?

"What is your decision?" she asked. "Do you choose to die or do you choose to marry me?"

As Ruth waited for his answer, an idea began to form in his mind.

A powerful idea.

An evil idea.

Chapter 27

"What is your decision?" Ruth repeated coldly.

Die! Nicholas screamed to himself. I would rather die than marry you!

But he did not let his emotions show. He kept his face still, his eyes blank.

Ruth had played her game. She had deceived him, tricked him. She was not the pitiful, shy girl he thought she was.

But Nicholas could play her game, too. Only he had plans to change the rules until they suited him.

Nicholas stared down at Jason's body, as if considering his options. Then he met Ruth's gaze and smiled. "I will marry you."

But then I will kill you and take your money, he silently added. And with your money I will marry Rosalyn and buy her everything she deserves.

* * *

Ruth made all the wedding arrangements. Two days later she and Nicholas stood in the parlor with the minister.

She told the minister she was still grieving over the loss of her father and wanted a quiet ceremony. The minister's wife and Mrs. Baker were the only witnesses.

The minister began to read the marriage vows. Ruth repeated the vows after the minister in a strong, clear voice.

Nicholas smiled at her blandly. You think you have won, Ruth, Nicholas thought. I cannot wait to see the surprise on your face when you realize how short "till death do us part" really is.

The minister turned to Nicholas. Nicholas repeated the vows, keeping his voice neutral. He did not want Ruth to suspect what he had planned for her.

Then the minister asked Nicholas to present Ruth with a token of his love. Ruth told him she did not want a ring. She wanted the amulet.

Nicholas hated the thought of Rosalyn's most prized possession hanging around Ruth's neck. Touching her cold skin.

She will only wear the amulet a short time, he reminded himself. I will reclaim it when I kill her. Rosalyn will never know I used it to gain our legacy.

He took a deep breath and draped the silver chain around Ruth's neck.

"You may now kiss the bride," the minister said jovially.

Nicholas leaned toward Ruth. Then he jerked back.

Something was wrong with her face. The skin seemed to *move.*

Maggots. Nicholas realized tiny white maggots were swarming in and out of her nose and mouth. Crawling everywhere.

Ruth reached out for him and pulled his head down to hers.

Chapter 28

Ruth smiled, and her teeth turned black with decay. They fell to the floor with little *ping* sounds.

The flesh ripped away from her face in chunks. He could see her cheekbones and part of her skull. One of her eyes dangled from a bloody string.

Ruth puckered her lips.

I cannot kiss her, Nicholas thought. I cannot.

The vision faded. Ruth's appearance returned to normal.

"Kiss me, Nicholas." She said it sweetly. But Nicholas knew it was an order.

Just get through the ceremony. You will be through with her tonight, Nicholas told himself. She will be dead tonight.

Nicholas quickly brushed his lips over hers. Ruth's lips were cold—like the rest of her.

But they will be colder before tomorrow morning, Nicholas thought. And I will never again have to kiss them.

"I suppose you will let people know of your marriage," the minister said after he wished them well.

"Yes, we will," Ruth assured him. "I know we should have waited, but it was my father's last request that we marry."

Nicholas took her hand, forcing himself to play his role. "Yes," he added. "And we both felt it was important to honor his dying wish."

The minister nodded approvingly. "I am sure you two want to be alone," he said. He ushered his wife and Mrs. Baker to the door.

Nicholas felt relieved when they had all given their best wishes and he could shut the door behind him.

He turned to Ruth. "I brought a bottle of champagne up from your father's wine cellar. I thought we could make a toast."

"Oh, Nicky! That is wonderful!" Ruth gushed. "I will change my clothes and be right back." She hurried across the room to the stairs.

Nicky. I hate that name, Nicholas thought as he made his way to the kitchen. I hate the way Ruth is smiling and acting like a silly little girl.

She knows I saw her grind the poker into Jason's throat. She knows I saw the horrible way she killed Betsy. Why is she bothering to pretend?

He glanced out the kitchen window. It was going to storm soon, he noticed.

Nicholas grabbed two glasses. He pulled a packet of rat poison out of his pocket and emptied it into one of them. Then he filled the glass with champagne and stirred until the poison dissolved.

The clerk at the feed store in Waynesbridge had assured him the packet was more than enough to handle all his rodent problems.

If the poison could kill all the rats in a barn, it could kill Ruth.

Nicholas filled his own glass, picked up Ruth's, and carried them to the study. Then he settled himself in one of the leather chairs to wait for Ruth.

The sky grew dark as more thunderclouds rolled in. Then it started to pour.

"You look so serious, Nicky," Ruth scolded. "What are you thinking about?"

Nicholas turned his head and found her standing in the doorway. She held a small wedding cake in her hands.

Lightning flashed, and the blue gems of the amulet around Ruth's throat glittered.

Time to play the game, Nicholas told himself.

He forced a bright smile. "I was just thinking how fortunate it was that I came to Shadyside."

Smiling, Ruth placed the cake on the desk. Then she circled behind his chair and rested her hands on his shoulders. "How sweet of you to realize so early in our marriage that you will be happy with me."

Nicholas tilted his head back and forced himself to gaze into those dead black eyes of hers. "You were right, Ruth. We are friends. We will be good company for each other."

Nicholas stood. "Let's have our toast."

Be careful, he told himself. Ruth is smart. If she notices you acting strange, it is over. She can still tell the police you murdered Jason.

Nicholas handed a glass to Ruth, then picked up his own. His hands did not shake. Good.

"I have never had champagne before, Nicky," Ruth exclaimed. "This is so much fun."

"I am glad you are having your first drink with me," Nicholas told her. Because then Ruth would not notice if the champagne tasted odd.

Nicholas raised his glass. "To our marriage!"

He started to take a sip.

"No!" Ruth cried.

He froze. "What is wrong?" he asked.

"We have to link arms. Then I drink out of your glass, and you drink out of mine. I read about it in a novel." Ruth moved closer and wrapped her arm around his.

The glass with the poison was inches from Nicholas's lips. His heart gave a little flutter in his chest. What could he do?

A knock sounded in the distance.

Saved! "I will answer it," Nicholas said loudly.

They untangled their arms, and Nicholas set his glass on the desk.

Tonight will no doubt be the longest night of my life, he thought as he hurried to the door. He planned to bury Ruth in the woods after he killed her. He had the hole all ready.

The knock sounded again.

Nicholas grabbed the handle and swung open the door.

He felt his heart drop. His throat went dry.

"Rosalyn," he whispered hoarsely.

Chapter 29

Nicholas rushed onto the porch and shut the door behind him.

Rosalyn wrapped her arms around his neck, and he held her close.

Her clothes were drenched, but he could feel the warmth of her body against his. Warm. So warm.

Nothing like Ruth's cold flesh. Nicholas shuddered, thinking about Ruth holding him in her arms.

Nicholas pressed his face into Rosalyn's wet hair. The scent of roses filled his nostrils. He wanted to forget Ruth. Forget all the death he had witnessed.

He never wanted to let Rosalyn go. But he had to. He could not allow Rosalyn to see Ruth. Rosalyn would never understand. He would lose her forever.

Nicholas moved back a step and stared down into Rosalyn's face, trying to memorize every detail. It felt as if years had gone by since they said good-bye on the train platform in Shadow Cove.

Only a few days had passed. But so much had happened. Too much.

Lightning flashed. Nicholas could clearly see the worry in Rosalyn's brown eyes. "Something is wrong," she said quietly. "Tell me."

"I want to tell you," Nicholas answered. "But I cannot. Not here. You must go. Take a room in the hotel. I will come for you tonight. I promise."

As soon as I kill my wife, he thought. Just as soon as I kill my wife.

Before Rosalyn could ask him a single question, Nicholas lowered his head and kissed her. Trying to show her how much he had missed her. How much he wanted to be with her. How much he loved her.

Then Nicholas gently pulled himself away from her. "You have to leave now."

Rosalyn nodded. "I love you, Nicholas."

The door behind Nicholas burst open. Light poured across the porch.

Ruth hurried up to Nicholas and grabbed his hand. "Oh, hello!" she cried to Rosalyn. "Are you one of Nicky's friends?"

Nicholas knew Rosalyn was waiting for him to introduce her as his fiancée. But he felt frozen. Unable to speak.

"I am Rosalyn," she answered finally.

Say something, Nicholas ordered himself. Anything. "Rosalyn needed directions to the hotel," he blurted out. "She has to leave right away."

"No!" Ruth protested. "Your friend must stay and join us for our toast. Since she was not in time for the wedding."

Nicholas saw the blood drain from Rosalyn's cheeks. Her face went chalk white.

"Impossible," Nicholas said weakly. "Rosalyn really must go to—"

Ruth ignored him. She linked arms with Rosalyn and led her into the house. Nicholas followed behind them. "I am so silly," Ruth chattered. "I did not introduce myself. I am Ruth. Mrs. Nicholas Fear."

Ruth glanced back at Nicholas. "Get another glass," she said, her black eyes expressionless.

"Rosalyn does not want to—" Nicholas began.

"No," Rosalyn interrupted. She turned to face him. "I want to toast your happiness. You know how important your happiness is to me, Nicholas."

Nicholas could hear the pain in Rosalyn's voice as she fought to stay in control.

"I will be right back with the glass," Nicholas mumbled. He hurried to the kitchen. His hands shook as he pulled another champagne glass down from the cupboard and filled it.

He had to get back to Rosalyn and Ruth. He had to make sure Rosalyn did not drink from the glass with the poison in it.

Nicholas made his way to the study as quickly as possible.

"See what Nicky gave me as a token of his love?" he heard Ruth boast as he entered the room.

"Nicholas must love you very much to give you

such a special gift," Rosalyn said quietly. She glanced at Nicholas and he saw tears filling her eyes.

He wanted to explain everything right away. But he could not. His plan had gone too far. Nicholas had to play the role of contented husband until Ruth was dead.

"Let's have our toast," Ruth said. She held up her glass.

Her glass.

Ruth already held a glass of the champagne.

So did Rosalyn.

But which glass held the poison?

Chapter 30

"To Nicholas and his new bride," Rosalyn said, holding her glass up.

Rosalyn brought the glass to her lips.

"Noooo!" Nicholas cried.

But Rosalyn drained the glass.

So did Ruth.

"What is wrong, Nicky?" Ruth chirped. "Did you want to make the toast?"

Nicholas ignored her. He stared back and forth between Ruth and Rosalyn. Who drank the poison?

"I will leave you two alone now," Rosalyn said.

"Won't you stay for a slice of wedding cake?" Ruth asked. She held up a large knife, ready to cut Rosalyn a piece.

"No. I must go."

Ruth shrugged and returned the knife to the cake plate.

Rosalyn took two steps toward the door. Then stumbled.

She took another step, and her knees buckled. She fell to the floor.

Nicholas rushed over and knelt beside her. Tremors raced through her body. She uttered a low moan.

Nicholas gathered her into his arms. He held her tight. Trying to stop her from shaking. "I am sorry, Rosalyn. Please forgive me. I never meant to hurt you."

Rosalyn's lips moved. Nicholas leaned closer. Straining to hear her. But he could not.

Then she choked. Coughing and coughing. Gasping for breath.

Deep red blood sprayed out of her mouth.

Her body stiffened.

Then went limp. Limp and still.

Dead.

Nicholas rocked back and forth, back and forth. Cradling Rosalyn's body.

Then he smoothed her black hair away from her face. He wiped the blood from her lips. "I am so sorry. I am so sorry, Rosalyn."

He repeated his apology over and over, even though she could not hear him. Would never again hear him.

With each passing moment, Rosalyn grew colder. "I love you," Nicholas murmured.

"You have to get rid of the body," Ruth said calmly.

Nicholas had forgotten she was in the room. Ruth should be dead, he thought. She is the one who is supposed to be dead. Not Rosalyn.

Ruth! he repeated to himself. Ruth was supposed to die.

Ruth will die.

The game will end now.

Nicholas leapt up. He grabbed the large knife on the cake plate.

And charged at Ruth.

Chapter 31

Ruth held the amulet up in front of her. Nicholas came to a dead stop.

The amulet glowed with a blue light.

"W-what?" Nicholas stammered.

Ruth laughed. "You do not even know what you have here. This amulet holds power. All the power you desire."

Ruth's voice was low and strong. She had let her mask slip again. Revealing the coldness that lay underneath.

"I understand the power, but I am not a Fear. So I cannot use the power the way you can. Imagine what we could do together," Ruth said.

"Power," Nicholas snarled. "I am about to teach you a lesson in power."

"Let me teach you first," Ruth said calmly. "This

amulet has been in the Fear family for generations. Daniel Fear gave it to Nora Goode when he married her."

Nicholas shook his head. "My mother did not give me the amulet. Rosalyn did. She found it on the beach when she was a child."

Ruth shrugged lightly. "The amulet is drawn to the Fears. My nurse used to work at the Fear mansion. She told me many tales about your family."

Nicholas stared at the pulsing blue light. He touched one of the amulet's silver claws. The metal felt warm under his fingers.

"You can feel its power, can't you, Nicholas? That power can be yours—with my help," Ruth urged.

He glanced at Ruth. Her dead black eyes revealed nothing.

I did not have to marry Ruth, Nicholas realized. The power was mine all along. I can still kill her. I can kill her right now.

"I know what you are thinking, Nicholas," Ruth said quietly. "You think you can have the power you crave without me. You are thinking about murdering me."

Nicholas's fingers tightened around the knife. "Why shouldn't I? After all you have done to me." He gazed down at Rosalyn's still body.

"*For* you!" Ruth protested. "I've done everything for you. You wanted power. Now you have it. I can teach you to harness it and to use it. Rosalyn would have stopped you from using your power."

Nicholas loosened his hold on the knife. Ruth was right. Rosalyn never would have approved of a power gained through evil.

"You and I can control the power," Ruth continued, her fingers wrapped around the amulet. "You are a Fear. I have learned everything I could about the amulet and the dark arts. Together we can have everything."

Rosalyn is dead, Nicholas thought.

My mother is dead.

I have no friends.

Why shouldn't I have power? It is all that is left for me.

Ruth knows I do not love her. I never will. But I can use her to get what I want.

Nicholas extended the knife toward Ruth.

"I think you were about to cut us a piece of wedding cake," he said.

Returning his smile, Ruth slipped her arm through his. "We have many plans to make, my husband."

Nicholas took one last glance at Rosalyn. Sweet, dead Rosalyn. Then he turned back to Ruth. "Many plans," he agreed.

I am a Fear, Nicholas thought. I will live my life as a Fear.

"Power through evil," he said. And smiled.

Epilogue

The people of Shadyside clapped as Nicholas used large scissors to cut the red ribbon. He and Ruth led the way onto a freshly cleared lot of land.

"This is the site for the first house on Fear Street," Nicholas announced. The crowd cheered.

Ruth moved up close behind him. Nicholas forced himself not to flinch when she ran her cold hand down his cheek. "I have a surprise for you," she whispered. "I am carrying your child."

A child.

Nicholas promised himself the child would grow up with all the things Nicholas never had. The child would have all the power and wealth of the Fear family.

"Together, we shall make Fear Street all it was

meant to be," Ruth vowed. She ran her fingers over the words engraved on the back of the amulet. POWER THROUGH EVIL.

Nicholas gazed over at the remains of the Fear mansion. Yes, he thought. Soon everyone will know the name of Fear Street.

About the Author

"Where do you get your ideas?"

That's the question that R. L. Stine is asked most often. "I don't know where my ideas come from," he says. "But I do know that I have a lot more scary stories in my mind that I can't wait to write."

So far, he has written nearly five dozen mysteries and thrillers for young people, all of them bestsellers.

Bob grew up in Columbus, Ohio. Today he lives in an apartment near Central Park in New York City with his wife, Jane, and son, Matt.

The Fear family has many dark secrets.
The family curse has touched many lives.
Discover the truth about them all in the

FEAR STREET SAGAS®

Next . . .

HOUSE OF WHISPERS

(Coming in mid-May 1996)

Amy Pierce has heard the rumors about her cousin Angelica Fear. She knows that people believe Angelica practices the dark arts. But Amy thinks that the people are just jealous. Jealous of Angelica's wealth and beauty.

Until Amy goes to stay with Angelica in her New Orleans mansion. From the moment Amy arrives she senses something wrong in the huge house. And death after death occurs.

Is her cousin responsible? If she is, how can Amy fight Angelica's evil powers all alone?